ARE YOU STILL CONFUSED?

FIND CLARITY, MOTIVATION & YOUR TRUE PATH

PUSHPA BHATTI

To every soul who has ever sat in silence, feeling lost, broken, or not
enough—
This book is for you.

To the girls told they're too emotional, the boys who were never allowed to
cry, and the women who kept going when no one clapped—
This is your mirror, your comfort, your fire.

And to my younger self—
You were never weak for feeling deeply. You were preparing to lead with
heart.

Contents

FOREWORD

There comes a time in every person's life when silence grows loud, when questions pile up, and the mirror reflects more doubt than clarity. It is in those fragile moments—when you whisper to yourself, "Am I the only one feeling this lost?"—that a book like this can be the light in your fog.

Are You Still Confused? isn't just a book. It's a conversation. A warm cup of chai shared between two souls. It's the friend who sits with you in your mess and says, "It's okay, I've been there too."

Pushpa Bhatti writes not from a pedestal but from lived experience. Her words are soaked in honesty, courage, and deep empathy. She doesn't offer quick fixes or lofty advice. Instead, she gently walks beside you—through confusion, heartbreak, inner battles, and quiet victories. This book holds space for your tears, your questions, your growth.

As you turn each page, I hope you feel less alone. I hope you rediscover your strength. I hope you start believing again—in yourself, in your journey, and in the quiet magic of becoming.

This book will not change your life in a single moment. But it will leave footprints on your heart that guide you home—to yourself.

So, take a deep breath. You're right where you need to be.
Let's begin.

— A Friend Who Believes in You

Preface

I didn't set out to write a book.

I set out to understand myself.

There were days I felt completely lost—torn between who I was and who I wanted to become. I saw the same confusion in the eyes of my friends, in the stories of students I mentored, and in the quiet silence of strong women who smiled through their struggles. Somewhere between all the roles, expectations, and pressures... I heard a question echo again and again:

"Am I enough? Will I ever find clarity?"

This book is born from that question.

Are You Still Confused? is not here to give you all the answers. It's here to hold your hand while you ask the right questions. It's a journey of messy truths, silent battles, soft breakdowns, and small wins. It's for the ones who want to heal but don't know where to start. The ones who carry strength they've never been taught to see.

Every chapter is a conversation—with your doubts, with your dreams, with the version of you that's still trying to believe she's worthy.

If you're holding this book, you don't need fixing.

You need space to feel, to process, to grow—and to rise.

This is my truth, written for yours.

Let's walk together—from confusion to clarity, from chaos to calm.

With all my heart,

Pushpa Bhatti

Acknowledgements

To the silent prayers, sleepless nights, and the little voice within me that never gave up — thank you.

This book was not written in isolation. It was born from real stories, raw emotions, and the quiet strength of those who believed in me when I couldn't believe in myself.

To every woman and youth who feels lost but still gets up each morning — you are the heartbeat of this book. Your strength inspired these pages.

To my family — thank you for your love and patience. Your support has been my grounding force.

To my friends and mentors — your words, encouragement, and sometimes just your presence were more powerful than you know.

To every soul who walks with silent struggles, hidden tears, and untold dreams — this is for you. You are not alone.

And to my younger self — thank you for surviving everything that was meant to break you. This book is the gift you deserved back then.

With deep love and infinite gratitude,
Pushpa Bhatti

I

The Fog of Confusion

1.1 Understanding Confusion

Have you ever felt like you're standing in the middle of a room full of people and still feel completely invisible?

You laugh, talk, smile — but inside, you feel blank. You get through the day, but your heart isn't in it. Your mind is constantly racing — thinking a thousand thoughts, asking endless questions — but getting no clear answers.

That's confusion.

It doesn't always come in dramatic forms. Sometimes, it's just silence. A pause in your energy. A heaviness in your chest. A voice in your head that quietly whispers:

"What am I even doing with my life?"

The Real Nature of Confusion

Confusion isn't weakness. It's not a sign that you're failing.

Confusion is actually a signal.

It means something inside you has begun to question the world outside you.

It means your soul is waking up.

We've been conditioned to believe that we must always have clarity — about our career, our relationships, our next step — and if we don't, we're failing. But that's not true.

The fog you feel? It's part of your growth.

Confusion is the pause between what was and what will be.
It's uncomfortable, yes — but it's also sacred.
It's the space where self-discovery begins.

What Confusion Can Look Like:

You don't know what career path to choose — you're scared of making the "wrong" decision.

You're in a relationship or friendship, but it doesn't feel right anymore.

You have dreams — big ones — but no idea how to start.

You feel like you've lost yourself trying to please others — family, friends, society.

You smile and perform on the outside but are completely numb on the inside.

You're not lazy.
You're not ungrateful.
You're not broken.
You are evolving.

You're in a Transition — Not a Trap

Let this sink in: You're not lost. You're transitioning.

Just like a seed must crack open before it grows.

Just like night must come before dawn.
Confusion comes before clarity.
Darkness comes before light.
Stillness comes before a breakthrough.

The fact that you're even reading this means you're already on your way.

Raw Truth: Confusion Hurts Because It's Honest

We feel confused when the life we're living doesn't align with the life we truly desire.

Maybe you've been told what to do your whole life.
Maybe you were never allowed to think for yourself.
Maybe every time you tried to express your feelings, someone told you to "adjust," "be quiet," or "be strong."

And now...

Now you're sitting with all these unspoken thoughts, unmet dreams, and unanswered questions — and it's overwhelming.

That's not your fault.

But here's the beautiful truth:

It's not too late to start listening to your inner voice.

? Words From Me to You

This book isn't going to tell you what to do.

It's going to help you hear yourself clearly — maybe for the first time in years.

You don't need more pressure.

You need permission.

Permission to feel confused.

Permission to sit with it.

Permission to say, "I don't know right now — and that's okay."

Because one day soon, you will know.

And until then — I'm walking this journey with you.

1.2 Common Causes of Confusion in Youth and Women

Confusion is not just a simple cloud over your head; it's a tangled web woven by countless threads of pressure, expectation, emotion, and uncertainty. For youth and women, this web often feels heavier, tighter, and harder to break free from because society piles on extra layers of judgment, responsibility, and invisibility. Let's break down what fuels this fog inside you — the causes that don't get spoken about enough.

1. The Crushing Pressure to Choose the "Right" Path

From a young age, we hear it loud and clear: "Choose a good career. Make your parents proud. Don't waste time."

But here's the brutal truth: you're expected to decide your entire future when you don't even know who you really are yet.

You're standing at a crossroads blindfolded, with voices shouting directions from all sides — family, teachers, friends, society.

You try to listen. You try to please.

But inside, confusion churns.

Are you chasing your dream, or someone else's?

This pressure crushes your spirit, and the fear of making the "wrong" choice traps you in indecision.

2. The Invisible Weight of Balancing Dreams with Duty

Women, especially, grow up hearing the silent commands:

"Be responsible. Take care of family. Don't rock the boat."

Your dreams don't fit neatly into these boxes.

Want to start a business? Risky.

Want to study abroad? Selfish.

Want to say no? Rebellious.

So you carry a heavy invisible weight on your shoulders — the tug between "What I want" and "What's expected."

Every step toward your dream feels like a betrayal.

Every step back feels like giving up on yourself.

Confusion grows in the space where your heart wants one thing and the world expects another.

3. The Poisonous Comparison Trap

In the age of social media, the fog thickens because you're constantly bombarded with others' highlight reels.

"Look at her success."

"Look at their happiness."

"Look at how perfect their life is."

You scroll and scroll, feeling smaller, slower, less than.

But here's the ugly truth no one tells you: social media is a carefully edited story. It's not reality.

You're measuring your behind-the-scenes with someone else's stage.

This comparison eats away your confidence, your joy, your clarity.

You lose sight of your own path because it doesn't look "like theirs."

4. The Silence Around Emotional Struggles

You're hurting. You want to speak out. But when you do, the response is often cold or dismissive:

"You're overthinking."

"Toughen up."

"Everyone has problems."

So you stop sharing. You lock your feelings inside.

Your confusion turns into loneliness, anxiety, maybe even depression.

You feel like you're carrying a heavy load alone — and that weight makes every decision harder.

5. Unhealed Wounds and Unspoken Pain

Past hurts don't magically disappear.

A harsh word, a betrayal, a loss — they embed themselves deep in your heart.

You try to move on, but those wounds whisper doubts and fears into your mind.

"How can I trust again?"

"Am I good enough?"

"Will I ever be happy?"

Confusion creeps in because your heart is still tangled in old pain. Healing is not linear — it's messy, slow, and painful. But necessary.

6. The Overwhelm of Being Multi-Passionate but Directionless

You're talented in many things. You're curious, creative, and capable. But society wants you to "choose one thing and stick to it."

That's easier said than done.

How do you decide when every interest feels like a piece of your soul? You want to write, but also help others.

You want to learn, but also create.

You want freedom, but also security.

So you freeze.

The fear of "choosing wrong" traps you in confusion and indecision.

7. The Fear of Judgment and Failure

Deep inside, you fear what people will say if you fail. You fear disappointing those who believe in you, or worse — being laughed at.

This fear paralyzes you.

You stay stuck in the fog because stepping forward feels like risking everything.

You become your own jailer, holding yourself back from the very life you want.

8. The Overload of Information and Opinions

We live in an age where advice is everywhere — books, videos, friends, experts.

Everyone has a different answer for "what you should do."

This noise drowns out your own voice.

You don't know what's right because you're caught in a storm of conflicting advice.

Remember: Your confusion is not a sign of weakness — it's a sign that you're growing, questioning, and evolving.

It's messy. It's painful.

But it's also the first step toward your own clarity and strength.

No matter how thick the fog feels today, there is a path forward.

You are not alone — and this journey is yours to own.

1.3 Why Confusion is a Natural Part of Growth

Confusion often feels like a curse — a dark cloud hovering over your mind, making every step uncertain and every choice heavy. But what if I told you confusion is actually a vital sign that you are growing? That beneath the chaos lies the powerful process of transformation?

Let's unpack why confusion is not your enemy, but your friend in disguise.

1. Confusion Means You're Questioning

When you feel lost or unsure, it means you're no longer accepting things as they are.

You're starting to question your beliefs, your choices, your environment, and most importantly — yourself.

This questioning is the seed of growth. It forces you to challenge old patterns and outdated ideas that no longer serve you.

Without confusion, there is no real reflection or change.

2. Growth Requires Leaving Your Comfort Zone

Growth is uncomfortable by nature.

Imagine a caterpillar inside its cocoon — it struggles, twists, and contorts before emerging as a butterfly. That confusion, that struggle, is necessary.

Your mind and soul are doing the same. They resist change because change is unknown and scary.

But confusion is the discomfort that precedes transformation.

3. Confusion is a Sign You're Exploring New Possibilities

When you're confused, it's because you're standing at a crossroads with many paths stretching out in front of you.

This means you're exploring new ideas, dreams, or ways of being. You are expanding your vision beyond what you've known.

The fog is just a temporary blur — soon, the clearer path will emerge as you explore and experiment.

4. Confusion Sparks Creativity and Innovation

Sometimes confusion pushes you to think differently.

It forces your brain to search for new solutions, new perspectives, and new ways to express yourself.

This discomfort can unlock creativity you never knew you had.

Many great ideas and breakthroughs come from times of confusion and uncertainty.

5. Confusion Builds Emotional Resilience

When you sit with confusion and discomfort, you learn to tolerate uncertainty.

This builds emotional strength and resilience.

You develop patience with yourself and your process.

You learn that it's okay to not have all the answers right now.

This patience will carry you through even tougher challenges in the future.

6. Confusion Invites You to Listen to Your Inner Voice

In the chaos of confusion, you are invited to turn inward.

You learn to listen beyond the noise of outside opinions, expectations, and pressures.

This quiet listening reveals your authentic desires and truths.

7. The Journey From Confusion to Clarity is a Path of Self-Discovery

The fog you're walking through is not the end — it's the beginning of discovering who you truly are and what you truly want.

Each step forward — even small and uncertain — is a step toward becoming more aligned with your real self.

Remember: Confusion is not failure. It is an essential part of your journey to self-awareness, growth, and empowerment.

It means you're alive, you're evolving, and you're ready to move forward — even if you don't yet see the full path.

1.4 Self-Assessment: Identifying Your Confusions

Before you can move forward and find clarity, you need to understand exactly where your confusion lies. This self-assessment is designed to help you gently explore your current state of mind and identify the areas where you feel most lost or uncertain.

Take your time with each question. Be honest with yourself — this is a safe space. There are no right or wrong answers, only your truth.

Reflect and Write:

What areas of your life feel most confusing right now?

Is it your career, relationships, personal identity, or future plans?

List the top 3 areas where you feel foggy or unsure.

What emotions come up when you think about these confusing areas?

Are you feeling fear, frustration, sadness, overwhelm, or something else?

Are there any decisions you are avoiding because of confusion?

Write down what decisions you find hard to make and why.

Do you notice any patterns in your confusion?

For example, does confusion arise when you think about certain people, situations, or choices?

What do you think is the biggest cause of your confusion?

Lack of information, fear of failure, external pressure, or something else?

How does your confusion affect your daily life?

Does it make you procrastinate, feel anxious, or avoid taking action?

When was the last time you felt clear and confident?

What was different then?

Be Specific

The clearer you are about your confusion, the easier it will be to work through it. Don't just say "I'm confused about my future." Try to describe what about your future is unclear — your job, your studies, your relationships, your self-worth?

Moving Forward

Once you finish this self-assessment, keep it somewhere safe. You will revisit your answers later in this book to track your progress.

Remember, identifying confusion is the first courageous step toward clarity and empowerment.

Tip:

If writing isn't your preferred way to express yourself, you can speak your answers aloud, record them on your phone, or discuss them with a trusted friend or mentor. The key is to bring your confusion into the light instead of letting it stay hidden in your mind.

Reflection Task: Your Current State of Mind

Take 10–15 minutes now to complete the self-assessment questions from section 3.4. Use a journal, notebook, or digital device—whatever feels comfortable.

Write honestly and openly.

Don't rush. Let your thoughts come naturally.

If you feel stuck, take a few deep breaths and return.

After completing the questions, pause and read what you wrote. Notice how it feels to bring your confusion out into the open. This is the first step to untangling the fog and starting your journey toward clarity.

Talk With the Reader: You're Not Alone in This Fog

Hey, I see you. Right now, it might feel like you're lost in thick fog—where every direction looks uncertain, and every step feels risky. That confusion you're carrying? It's real, it's heavy, and it's okay to feel overwhelmed.

But here's the truth: you are not alone. So many youth and women are walking the same foggy path, battling similar doubts and fears. The good news? This confusion is not your final destination—it's a necessary crossroads.

This fog means something beautiful is happening inside you—a process of growth, change, and awakening. It's messy and uncomfortable, yes. But on the other side lies clarity, strength, and the power to design your own path.

Hold on to this truth: the fog will lift. Step by step, word by word in this book, you'll begin to find your way out. And I'll be walking with you.

You've already taken the bravest step—acknowledging the confusion and being willing

to face it. Keep going. You are stronger than you know.

II

Chapter 2: Facing Your Struggles

2.1 Recognizing Your Struggles

Struggles are an inevitable part of life—especially during youth and in the journey of womanhood. They can come in many shapes and sizes: internal battles, external challenges, relationship issues, societal pressures, or moments of self-doubt and fear.

The first step to overcoming these struggles is to recognize them clearly. Sometimes, struggles hide behind a mask of "everything's fine" or "I can handle this," but ignoring them only gives them power over your life.

What Are Your Struggles?

Take a moment to reflect: what are the struggles that you face every day or have been avoiding? Maybe it's:

Feeling stuck in a career or education path

Pressure from family or society to conform

Emotional pain from past relationships or current conflicts

Self-esteem issues or imposter syndrome

Balancing personal dreams with responsibilities

Recognizing your struggles means admitting that they exist, without judgment or shame. It means giving yourself permission to feel the pain, frustration, or confusion that comes with them.

Why Is This Important?

Because you can't fix what you don't acknowledge. Hiding struggles in the dark creates more confusion and anxiety. When you bring them into the light, you begin to understand their impact—and that's where healing and growth start.

Remember: struggles do not make you weak. They make you human. They are part of your story, but they don't have to define your future.

2.2 Emotional Impact of Struggles

Struggles are rarely just about the external situations we face—they seep deep into our emotional core and shape how we see ourselves and the world around us. When you face hardships, your emotional landscape can become turbulent, affecting your thoughts, decisions, and even your physical health.

It's common to experience a rollercoaster of emotions when dealing with struggles: sadness that feels heavy and never-ending, anger that boils beneath the surface, confusion about what to do next, and sometimes, even despair or hopelessness that makes you question your purpose.

The Emotional Toll

These feelings are not signs of weakness or failure. They are natural, human responses to pain and uncertainty. For many youth and women, the pressure of societal expectations adds an extra layer of emotional complexity. You might feel like you have to be strong all the time, smile through the pain, or hide your true feelings to avoid being judged.

But bottling up emotions or denying their existence can have serious consequences:

Anxiety and Restlessness: Your mind may race with worries and fears about the future, making it difficult to concentrate or enjoy simple moments.

Mood Swings: You might feel happy one moment and deeply upset the next, confused by the unpredictability of your own emotions.

Self-Doubt: Struggles often shake your confidence. You may start questioning your abilities, your worth, and your potential.

Isolation: When emotions become intense, it can feel like no one truly understands your experience, leading to feelings of loneliness and disconnection.

Why It's Important to Feel

While the pain may feel unbearable, trying to suppress or ignore these emotions will not make them disappear. Instead, they tend to build up inside, sometimes manifesting as physical symptoms like headaches, fatigue, or even illness.

Allowing yourself to truly feel your emotions is a form of self-respect and self-care. When you give yourself permission to be vulnerable, you open the door to healing.

Crying is Healing: Tears can release stress and cleanse emotional wounds.

Expressive Writing Helps: Putting your feelings into words clarifies your thoughts and lightens emotional burdens.

Talking Matters: Sharing your struggles with a trusted friend, mentor, or counselor can provide relief and perspective.

Harnessing Emotional Awareness

Developing emotional awareness is a skill that helps you navigate your struggles with greater ease. Instead of being overwhelmed or controlled by your feelings, you learn to recognize them as signals—alerts from your inner self that something needs attention.

This awareness allows you to:

Pause before reacting impulsively

Understand the root causes of your emotions

Choose healthy ways to cope, such as meditation, exercise, or creative outlets

Build emotional resilience that strengthens you for future challenges

Remember, emotional growth doesn't happen overnight. It is a gradual process, often requiring patience and kindness toward yourself. But every step you take to honor your feelings brings you closer to inner peace and confidence.

2.3 The Role of Struggles in Building Strength

Struggles are often viewed as obstacles that block our path or burdens that weigh us down. But what if we changed the way we see them? What if struggles are not just hardships to endure, but powerful catalysts that shape us into stronger, more resilient human beings?

Life doesn't promise an easy road. Every person, no matter who they are, will face struggles at some point. The difference lies in how we respond to these struggles — whether we allow them to defeat us, or whether we use them to build strength and move forward.

Why Struggles Are Essential for Growth

Imagine a seed planted in soil. For it to sprout and grow into a tall tree, it must push through the dark earth. Without resistance, the seed would never break open and begin life. Similarly, struggles act as resistance that challenges us to grow, to break out of our shells, and to stretch beyond our limits.

Struggles push us into discomfort, and it is in this discomfort that growth happens. When you face difficulties, you're forced to confront fears, doubts, and weaknesses that may have been hidden beneath the surface. It's a process that strips away illusions and reveals your true strength.

The Transformative Power of Struggle

Struggles test your patience, your courage, and your commitment. But through these tests, you learn invaluable lessons:

Patience: When progress is slow and obstacles keep appearing, struggle teaches you to wait, to endure, and to trust the process.

Perseverance: It shows you that giving up is not an option if you want to reach your goals.

Self-Discipline: Struggle demands consistent effort even when motivation is low.

Problem-Solving: Challenges push your mind to think creatively and develop new solutions.

Humility: Facing struggles reminds you that you don't have all the answers, and that seeking help or learning from others is a strength, not a weakness.

Struggles Build Emotional and Mental Resilience

Resilience is the ability to bounce back from adversity. It's not about never falling down, but about getting up every time with more wisdom and strength. Struggles are like workouts for your emotional muscles — they stretch you, tire you, but ultimately make you tougher.

When you look back on your past struggles, you might see how they prepared you for future challenges. Maybe a failure taught you humility and planning. Maybe a heartbreak taught you how to love yourself better. Maybe a loss taught you the value of gratitude.

Real-Life Examples: Strength Through Struggle

Some of the world's most inspiring figures faced overwhelming struggles before rising to greatness. Their stories show that strength is forged in the fire of hardship:

Nelson Mandela spent 27 years in prison but emerged as a leader who united a divided nation.

Helen Keller lost her sight and hearing but became a powerful advocate for people with disabilities.

Thomas Edison failed thousands of times before inventing the light bulb, refusing to see failure as the end.

These examples remind us that struggle is not the opposite of success — it is a vital part of the journey to success.

How Struggles Shape Your Identity

Struggles don't just make you stronger — they shape who you are. They clarify what matters most and help you find purpose. You begin to understand your values more deeply and learn what you truly want in life.

Each struggle faced and overcome adds a new layer to your character. You develop qualities like courage, empathy, wisdom, and determination. These qualities become your foundation, your inner armor to face future storms.

Learning to Embrace Struggle

No one wants to suffer, but avoiding struggle is impossible. Instead of fearing difficulties, learn to embrace them as opportunities for growth. This shift in mindset is powerful:

When you face a problem, instead of asking "Why me?" ask "What can I learn from this?"

When you feel overwhelmed, remind yourself that this moment is temporary and that strength will come.

Celebrate small victories over struggles, because each one is a step forward.

Practical Tips to Use Struggles to Build Strength

Reflect on Past Challenges: Write down past struggles and how you overcame them. What strengths did you discover in yourself?

Practice Gratitude: Find things to be grateful for, even in difficult times. Gratitude shifts your focus from pain to progress.

Seek Support: Strength doesn't mean going it alone. Find mentors, friends, or counselors who can support you through tough times.

Set Small Goals: Break down your struggles into manageable tasks. Celebrate each small success to build confidence.

Develop Healthy Coping Mechanisms: Exercise, meditation, journaling, or creative activities can help you process struggles healthily.

In the end, struggles are not punishments or signs of failure. They are the raw material from which strength, courage, and success are built. Remember, the strongest steel is forged in the hottest fire. Your struggles are shaping you — trust the process, and keep moving forward.

2.4 Reflection Exercise: Writing About Your Struggles

Writing about your struggles is one of the most powerful tools you have for healing and growth. When you put your thoughts and feelings into words, you give yourself permission to confront what's inside and make sense of it. This process helps you release the burden of confusion, frustration, and pain, and gradually transform it into clarity and strength.

Why Writing Helps

Many people underestimate the power of writing, but journaling or reflection exercises can unlock deep insights and provide emotional relief. Writing acts like a mirror, showing you the patterns of your thoughts and feelings. It helps you recognize what's really bothering you, what fears are holding you back, and what hopes you still carry.

When you write about your struggles, you create a safe space just for you. You don't have to hide, explain, or justify anything. Your words belong to you alone, and they are a truthful expression of your inner world.

How to Approach This Exercise

This reflection exercise is not about perfection or grammar. It's about honesty and vulnerability. Give yourself permission to write whatever comes up, without censoring or judging your thoughts. The goal is not to produce a masterpiece but to open your heart and mind.

You can write by hand in a notebook or type on your phone or computer—choose whatever feels most comfortable and private for you.

Step-by-Step Guide for Writing About Your Struggles

Find a Quiet Space: Choose a place where you feel safe and won't be interrupted. This helps you focus on your feelings and thoughts.

Set a Timer: Start with 10-15 minutes. You can extend the time if you feel inspired, but don't pressure yourself to write long.

Start Writing Freely: Begin by writing about what is currently troubling you. It can be a specific event, a feeling, or even confusion about what you want.

Be Honest: Let your true emotions flow. If you feel angry, sad, scared, or lost, write it down. Don't hold back.

Ask Yourself Questions: If you get stuck, try asking yourself:

What am I really feeling right now?

What is the hardest part of this struggle for me?

How have these struggles affected my life?

What do I want to change or understand better?

Reflect on Your Strengths: After expressing the pain, write about any small victories or strengths you have discovered through this struggle.

End With Compassion: Finish your writing session by acknowledging that it's okay to struggle and reminding yourself that growth takes time.

What You May Experience

At first, writing about your struggles can feel uncomfortable or even overwhelming. That's normal. You may uncover emotions you have buried deep inside. But remember, facing these feelings is the first step toward healing.

Over time, this practice can help you:

Feel lighter by releasing pent-up emotions.

Gain clarity on what you really want and need.

Develop self-awareness about your patterns and triggers.

Build resilience and confidence in your ability to face challenges.

Example Journal Prompt to Get You Started

"Today, I want to write about the struggle that weighs heaviest on my heart. I will describe how it feels, what thoughts come to my mind, and how it affects my daily life. I will also try to see if there is any lesson or strength hidden in this struggle."

Your Turn: Reflection Writing Task

Take out your journal or open a blank document. Set your timer and begin your writing. Don't worry about structure or making sense. Just write your truth. If you want, revisit your writing later to notice how your feelings and thoughts evolve.

Remember, this exercise is a gift you give yourself — a chance to understand and heal from your struggles. You are not alone, and every word you write is a step forward on your journey to strength.

III

Finding the First Spark

3.1 Moments of Hope and Inspiration

In the darkest and most confusing phases of life, when everything feels heavy and uncertain, hope often seems like a faint glimmer—almost impossible to grasp. Yet, it is precisely these tiny flickers of hope that hold the potential to turn your life around. They can appear in the most unexpected ways: a comforting word from a stranger, a story of someone who triumphed against all odds, a quiet moment of clarity during chaos, or even a simple smile from someone who understands your pain. These seemingly small moments have the extraordinary power to reignite your inner fire and remind you that you are not alone.

Hope is not about denying your struggles or pretending everything is perfect. It is about choosing to believe that no matter how hard life gets, there is a possibility for change, healing, and growth. It is the quiet strength that tells you, "This pain is temporary," and "There is a way forward." Hope is the anchor that keeps you grounded when the storms of doubt and fear rage within you.

Inspiration often comes hand in hand with hope. It might be sparked by a book that speaks to your soul, a song whose lyrics echo your unspoken feelings, or witnessing a sunrise after a long night filled with worries. These moments awaken a part of you that longs for something better, something meaningful. They fuel your desire to move beyond confusion and despair, to dream again, and to believe in your own potential.

Recognizing these moments requires openness and presence. When you're overwhelmed by negative thoughts or tangled in confusion, these sparks can be easy to miss or dismiss. But once you start paying attention—once you learn to notice the small signs of hope and inspiration—they become lifelines, guiding you out of darkness and into a place of possibility.

Every great journey begins with a spark—a moment when you decide that you want more for yourself. It could be the memory of a childhood dream, a quiet affirmation whispered in your mind, or the courage to take one small step toward change. This spark is your first glimpse of clarity, the start of your transformation.

Remember, hope and inspiration don't have to come in grand gestures. Often, they live in the quiet, everyday moments: the gentle touch of a loved one's hand, the encouragement from a friend, or the resilience you see in yourself after surviving a tough day. These moments build up, layer by layer, creating the foundation for your strength and determination.

So, hold on to those sparks. Protect them, nurture them, and let them grow. When you do, you'll find that even in the midst of confusion, there is always light—and within that light, you will find your way.

3.2 Nurturing Your Inner Spark

Once you have recognized those precious moments of hope and inspiration—the sparks within you—the next crucial step is to nurture them. Your inner spark is like a fragile flame that needs care, attention, and protection from the harsh winds of doubt, fear, and negativity. When nurtured, this spark grows stronger, becoming a powerful source of motivation and resilience that can carry you through even the toughest times.

Nurturing your inner spark begins with self-awareness. It requires tuning in to what truly moves you, excites you, and brings you joy. Ask yourself: What are the things that make your heart beat faster? What dreams or passions do you secretly hold? Sometimes, these answers might be buried beneath layers of confusion or fear, but they are there, waiting patiently for you to rediscover them.

Self-care is a vital part of nurturing your spark. This means prioritizing your mental, emotional, and physical well-being. When you take time to rest, recharge, and do things that bring you peace, you create space for your spark to grow. This might include journaling your thoughts, meditating, spending time in nature, or engaging in creative activities like drawing, music, or writing. These practices connect you back to yourself and your deeper desires.

Another important way to nurture your inner spark is by surrounding yourself with positivity. This includes the people you interact with, the books you read, the media you consume, and the environment you live in. Seek out mentors, friends, or communities that uplift you, encourage your growth, and support your dreams. Distance yourself from negativity and toxic influences that drain your energy or dim your light.

Nurturing your spark also means setting small, manageable goals that keep your motivation alive. These goals don't have to be huge or intimidating. Even the smallest achievements, like waking up with a positive affirmation, completing a task, or learning something new, feed your spark and build your confidence. Celebrate these victories, no matter how minor they may seem, because each step forward fuels your inner fire.

Remember, nurturing your spark is a continuous process. There will be days when your flame flickers and seems weak—this is natural. Be gentle with yourself during these times. Instead of judging or pushing too hard, acknowledge where you are, give yourself permission to rest, and remind yourself that your spark is still there, waiting to be reignited.

Your inner spark is a gift—your unique light that guides you toward your purpose and dreams. Protect it, nurture it, and trust that it will grow stronger with every act of love and care you give yourself. When you nurture your spark, you're not only investing in your future success but also in your healing and transformation.

3.3 Setting Small Achievable Goals

Setting goals is essential for turning your dreams and hopes into reality. However, the key is to start small. When we're confused or overwhelmed, aiming too high or setting unrealistic goals can backfire, leading to frustration and giving up. Instead, setting small, achievable goals allows you to build momentum, gain confidence, and create a clear path forward.

Small goals act like stepping stones that gradually take you closer to your bigger vision. For example, if your dream is to start a career or a business, a small goal could be updating your resume, researching the industry, or connecting with one new person in your field. These tasks might seem minor, but they add up to significant progress over time.

When setting your goals, use the SMART framework:

Specific: Be clear about what exactly you want to achieve.

Measurable: Define how you will know you've achieved it.

Achievable: Set goals that are realistic and within your reach.

Relevant: Make sure your goals align with your values and dreams.

Time-bound: Give yourself a deadline to create urgency and focus.

Writing down your goals makes them more real and keeps you accountable. Break down each goal into small, actionable steps. Instead of saying, "I want to be confident," say, "I will practice speaking up in one meeting this week." Small, concrete actions create a sense of accomplishment and encourage you to keep going.

Remember, the journey of a thousand miles begins with a single step. Celebrate each small win, no matter how insignificant it may seem. These wins are proof of your dedication and capability. Don't compare your progress with others; focus on your path and your pace.

Goal-setting is not a one-time event. Regularly review and adjust your goals based on your experiences and evolving dreams. Flexibility allows you to stay motivated even when life throws challenges your way.

By setting small achievable goals, you build confidence, reduce confusion, and create clarity. You begin to see your dreams taking shape step by step, making the journey less daunting and more exciting.

3.4 Goal-Setting Worksheet

To help you put everything into practice, here is a simple worksheet you can use to set and track your goals. Take your time and be honest with yourself. This exercise will help you break down your dreams into clear, manageable steps.

Step 1: Define Your Big Goal

What is one big goal or dream you want to work towards?

Step 2 Break It Down Into Smaller Goals

Write down 3-5 small goals or milestones that will help you reach your big goal. Make sure they are specific and achievable.

Step 3: Identify Actionable Steps

For each small goal, write down at least 2 actions you will take.

Small Goal 1:

Action 1:

Action 2:

Small Goal 2:

Action 2:

(Repeat as needed)

Step 4: Set Deadlines

Give yourself realistic deadlines for each small goal and action.

Small Goal 1 Deadline:

Small Goal 2 Deadline:

(Add more as needed)

Step 5: Celebrate Your Wins

Plan how you will reward yourself when you achieve each small goal. Celebrate every step forward!

Reflection

How do you feel about your goals now?

What challenges do you anticipate?

How can you stay motivated during setbacks?

Use this worksheet as a living document—review and update it regularly as you progress. Remember, goal-setting is a powerful tool to transform confusion into clarity and action.

IV

Battling Inner Demons

It's okay to have moments of uncertainty. Everyone does. The goal is to not let those moments freeze you in place. When self-doubt whispers, listen with compassion, then remind yourself of your strengths and past successes. You are more capable than you think — and every step you take is proof of your courage.

4.3 Techniques to Replace Negative Thoughts

Negative thoughts can feel like heavy chains that hold you back from moving forward. They often come uninvited, repeating harsh criticisms or fears that chip away at your self-esteem and motivation. But the good news is: you have the power to recognize these thoughts and replace them with healthier, more constructive ones. This process takes effort and patience, but it's one of the most important steps toward emotional freedom and personal growth.

Why It's Important to Replace Negative Thoughts

Our minds tend to focus on what's wrong — a survival mechanism rooted in evolution. But in today's world, this habit can cause unnecessary suffering. Negative thoughts affect your emotions, behavior, and even your physical health by increasing stress hormones. By actively working to replace negativity, you improve your mental clarity, build resilience, and create space for positivity and success.

Step 1: Recognize Your Negative Thoughts

The first step in changing your thinking is awareness. Negative thoughts often happen so quickly and unconsciously that they become automatic. You might catch yourself thinking:

"I'm not worthy of success."

"I'll never be able to do this."

"I always fail."

"Nobody cares about me."

Write these down when you notice them. Seeing your thoughts on paper makes them easier to confront.

Step 2: Question Your Thoughts — Challenge Their Truth

Now, critically examine these thoughts. Ask yourself:

Is this thought 100% true?

What proof do I have to support it?

Are there facts or experiences that contradict this thought?

Am I generalizing or jumping to conclusions?

Would I say this to someone I care about?

For example, if your thought is "I always fail," reflect on moments when you succeeded, even small ones. This helps you realize that your negative thoughts are often exaggerations or distortions.

Step 3: Reframe or Replace Negative Thoughts

Reframing means looking at the situation from a different, more positive angle. Instead of allowing harsh negativity, practice replacing thoughts with ones that are true but kinder and more hopeful.

Examples:

From "I'm a failure" to "I made a mistake, but I am learning and growing."

From "I can't handle this" to "This is tough, but I have overcome challenges before."

From "Nobody cares about me" to "Some people care deeply, and I am not alone."

This doesn't mean ignoring problems or pretending everything is perfect; it means balancing the negative with realistic and encouraging perspectives.

Step 4: Use Affirmations to Build Positive Thinking

Affirmations are simple positive statements that you repeat to yourself to help build new neural pathways in your brain. The more you say them, the more your mind starts to accept them as truth.

Examples:

"I am worthy of love and respect."

"I am capable of achieving my goals."

"I choose to focus on what I can control."

Create affirmations that resonate deeply with you. Write them on sticky notes or set reminders to repeat them daily.

Step 5: Practice Mindfulness and Meditation

Mindfulness teaches you to observe your thoughts without getting caught up in them. When a negative thought arises, acknowledge it gently, label it ("there's that worry again"), and let it drift away like a cloud. Meditation strengthens this ability to stay present and calm.

Regular practice can reduce the intensity and frequency of negative thoughts, allowing you to respond to them rather than react automatically.

Step 6: Visualize Positive Outcomes

Use the power of your imagination to picture yourself succeeding or handling difficult situations with confidence. Visualization rewires your brain to expect positive results.

For example, before a challenging event, close your eyes and imagine yourself staying calm, speaking clearly, and feeling proud afterward. This mental rehearsal boosts self-confidence and reduces anxiety.

Step 7: Cultivate Gratitude

Gratitude shifts your focus from what's lacking to what's abundant in your life. Each day, list at least three things you're grateful for — big or small. This simple practice changes brain chemistry by increasing dopamine and serotonin, the "feel-good" chemicals.

When you regularly acknowledge your blessings, negative thoughts lose their power and you become more optimistic and resilient.

Consistency and Patience Are Key

Changing the way you think is a journey, not an instant fix. You may find yourself slipping back into negative thought patterns occasionally — and that's okay. What matters is that you recognize it and bring yourself back on track. Over time, these new mental habits will become your natural way of thinking.

Remember: Your thoughts are not facts. They are just mental events that can be changed. You hold the pen to rewrite your inner story — with kindness, courage, and hope.

Talk With the Reader:

I know it's not easy to confront the negativity in your mind. It can feel like fighting an invisible enemy inside your head. But trust me — you are stronger than your thoughts. Every time you choose to challenge a negative belief and replace it with a positive one, you grow stronger. This is your path to freedom, peace, and your true potential.

6.4 Thought-Challenging Exercise

Changing negative thought patterns requires practice. This exercise will help you become more aware of your thoughts and actively challenge those that are harmful or untrue. You can do this daily or whenever you notice negativity creeping in.

Step 1: Identify the Negative Thought

Start by writing down a specific negative thought that has been bothering you. Be as precise as possible. For example:

"I am not good enough to get this job."

"I always mess up in social situations."

"No one understands me."

Step 2: Analyze the Evidence

Look at the facts. Ask yourself:

What evidence supports this thought?

What evidence contradicts it?

Are you relying on feelings rather than facts?

Write down both supporting and contradicting evidence. This step helps bring balance and reality to your thinking.

Step 3: Consider Alternative Perspectives

Challenge your initial thought by brainstorming at least two alternative, more balanced or positive perspectives. For example:

"I may not be perfect, but I have skills and experience that qualify me."

"Sometimes social situations are hard, but I have had good conversations before."

"Some people understand me, even if not everyone does."

Step 4: Replace the Negative Thought

Choose one of the alternative perspectives and write it down as a replacement for your negative thought. Make it positive, realistic, and encouraging. For example:

"I am capable and deserving of this opportunity."

"I am improving my social skills with each experience."

"I am surrounded by people who care about me."

Step 5: Reflect on How You Feel

After replacing your negative thought, pause and notice any changes in your feelings or mindset. Are you calmer, more hopeful, or motivated? Write a few words about your emotional shift.

Example Worksheet

Negative Thought

Evidence For

Evidence Against
Alternative Thoughts
New Thought
Emotional Impact
"I always fail."
I failed my last exam.
I passed previous exams. I've succeeded in other areas.
"Failure is part of learning." "I have succeeded before and can do it again."
"I am learning and growing from my experiences."
Hopeful, motivated
Tips for Success
Be patient with yourself — this is a skill that strengthens over time.
Don't judge your thoughts harshly; simply observe and challenge them.
Use this exercise whenever negative thoughts overwhelm you or affect your mood.

V
The Power of Consistency

5.1 Importance of Daily Habits

Consistency is the silent architect of success. It shapes your life not through sudden bursts of effort but through the power of repeated, small actions. Think of daily habits as the threads weaving the fabric of your future — each thread may seem insignificant alone, but together, they create something strong and beautiful.

Why do daily habits matter so much? Because habits shape your identity. When you do something consistently, it becomes part of who you are. This is the secret: you become what you repeatedly do. If you wake up every day determined to learn, no matter how little, you become a learner. If you show up for your health daily, you become a healthy person. The reverse is true too — negative habits become part of your identity if left unchecked.

One of the biggest challenges in achieving your goals is motivation. Motivation can be fleeting. You feel excited for a day or two, but then life's challenges distract you. This is where habits step in. When a behavior becomes a habit, it no longer relies on motivation. It becomes automatic, a natural part of your routine that you do without having to think hard about it. This helps you push through days when you feel tired, stressed, or uninspired.

Another reason daily habits are powerful is their cumulative effect. Just like how drops of water fill a bucket, small positive actions accumulate over time to create remarkable results. For example, reading 10 pages a day might seem small, but over a year, it could add up to reading dozens of books, transforming your knowledge and perspective. Saving a small amount of money every day can build a significant financial safety net. Consistency is the multiplier that turns small efforts into massive achievements.

Daily habits also create structure and stability in your life. When your days follow a positive routine, it reduces chaos and overwhelm. You start your day with clarity and purpose, instead of feeling lost or reactive. This structure boosts your confidence because you know you are taking control of your actions and decisions.

Moreover, daily habits foster discipline, which is the backbone of self-growth. Discipline isn't about harsh restrictions but about honoring your commitment to yourself. It teaches you patience, resilience, and the ability to delay gratification — essential qualities for long-term success.

It's important to remember that building habits is not about perfection. You will miss days, face setbacks, or get distracted — that's part of being human. The key is to get back on track without judgment. Over time, these small daily habits will become your foundation, supporting you through challenges and helping you reach your goals.

Practical Examples of Daily Habits to Build:

Starting your morning with a simple mindfulness or breathing exercise to calm your mind

Writing down three things you are grateful for every day

Spending 15 minutes on a hobby or skill that excites you

Drinking a glass of water first thing in the morning to hydrate your body

Setting a small goal for the day and reviewing your progress in the evening

Taking a short walk or stretching to energize your body

Avoiding social media for the first hour after waking up

Each of these actions might seem small on its own, but repeated daily, they shape a life filled with purpose, health, and growth.

Talk With the Reader:

Imagine looking back six months from now. What habits will you be grateful for having started today? Which small actions will have transformed your confidence, health, and mindset? The journey doesn't require giant steps, but it does require steady ones. Consistency might feel slow, but it's unstoppable. Your daily habits are your most loyal allies — nurture them, and watch your life change.

5.2 Building Momentum Through Small Steps

Let me be honest with you—sometimes, the hardest part of any journey is simply getting started. When everything feels confusing or overwhelming, thinking about the big picture can freeze you. You wonder, "Where do I even begin? How do I make this huge change?"

That's where small steps come in. They might seem insignificant at first, but they're the secret sauce to building real, lasting momentum. Imagine you want to change your life or reach a big goal. Instead of trying to do it all at once, just focus on one tiny thing you can do today. Maybe it's writing down one goal, or waking up five minutes earlier, or simply telling yourself, "I can try."

These small actions might look tiny, but they matter so much. They are like little sparks—when you keep adding spark after spark, you build a fire. When you take one small step, you prove to yourself that you can take action. And that feeling—that "I did something"—is powerful. It motivates you to take the next step.

Think of momentum like a gentle push on a swing. At first, it barely moves. But with each small push, the swing goes higher and higher. The same happens with your goals. Each small effort adds up. Before you know it, you're moving forward more easily and confidently than you thought possible.

Why is this so important? Because when you start with big leaps, it often feels too hard or exhausting. You might try to change everything at once, and then get overwhelmed and give up. But when you start small, it feels manageable. It doesn't drain your energy—it builds it. It helps you avoid burnout and keeps you steady.

Here's the truth: progress isn't about perfection. It's about showing up, even when you don't feel like it. Even on days when you feel stuck or tired, doing just a little bit is still moving forward. And that little bit adds up in ways you can't see right away.

Here are some ideas for taking those small steps:

Break your big dreams into tiny, doable tasks. Don't think about finishing the whole race—just focus on the next step.

Celebrate your wins, no matter how small. Finished writing one paragraph? That's a win. Chose a healthy meal today? That's progress.

Be kind to yourself if you miss a day or slip up. The important thing is to start again tomorrow.

Use simple tools to remind yourself—like setting a phone alarm or keeping a checklist.

Share your small wins with a friend or family member. Sometimes, just telling someone else can boost your motivation.

Remember, momentum isn't about rushing or pushing too hard. It's about being gentle with yourself and consistent. Little by little, day by day, those small steps turn into something big. A new habit, a new confidence, a new you.

Talk With the Reader:

I want you to hear this clearly: you don't need to have everything figured out right now. You don't have to make massive changes overnight. What matters is that you start—right where you are, with what you have. Take that tiny step today. Trust me, it's the start of something beautiful. And I promise, you're stronger than you think.

5.3 Creating Positive Habits

Creating positive habits isn't about forcing yourself or being perfect. It's about gently guiding your mind and body toward choices that serve you better — slowly, step by step. Think of habits like little investments in yourself. Every time you do something good for you, even if it feels small or simple, you're building a stronger foundation for your future.

Here's the thing: habits shape your daily life more than your motivation does. Motivation comes and goes like the weather—it's exciting one day and gone the next. Habits, on the other hand, become automatic. They don't rely on willpower or mood; they become part of who you are.

But how do you actually create these habits?

Start by choosing one habit that truly matters to you—something that feels meaningful or brings you peace, joy, or growth. Don't overwhelm yourself with a long list. One habit at a time is enough.

Then, make it easy to do. If you want to read more, keep a book beside your bed. If you want to drink more water, carry a water bottle with you. The easier it is to do, the more likely you'll stick with it.

Consistency beats intensity every single time. Doing a little bit every day—even if it's just five minutes—is more powerful than doing a lot once in a while.

Also, be patient with yourself. Habits don't form overnight. It takes time—sometimes weeks or months. There will be days you miss, and that's okay. What matters is that you get back on track without judgment or guilt.

Celebrate your progress, even the small wins. Each day you show up, you're training your brain to believe change is possible.

Remember, you're not trying to become a perfect person. You're simply becoming a better version of yourself, one small habit at a time.

Talk With the Reader:

I know change can feel scary or tiring. But imagine how it will feel when these new habits start to feel natural—when they become your daily rhythm and you don't have to think twice. That's freedom. That's growth. And it's completely within your reach. Take a deep breath, be kind to yourself, and keep moving forward.

5.4 Habit Tracker Template

Tracking your habits might sound like extra work, but it's actually one of the easiest ways to stay motivated and see your progress clearly. When you mark off each day you complete your habit, it creates a visual reminder of how far you've come — and that feels really good.

Here's a simple way to create your own habit tracker:

Step 1: Choose 1–3 habits you want to focus on this month. Keep it manageable.

Step 2: Create a calendar or chart with the days of the month listed.

Step 3: Each day, mark an X or a checkmark if you did your habit. If you miss a day, that's okay — just start fresh the next day.

Step 4: At the end of the week, reflect on what worked and what didn't. Adjust if needed, but don't give up.

Sample Habit Tracker Layout

Date

Habit 1 (e.g., Drink Water)

Habit 2 (e.g., Read 10 mins)

Habit 3 (e.g., Meditation)

1

√

√

2

√

√

3

√

√

Talk With the Reader:

I want you to know it's okay if you don't get a perfect streak. Life happens, and some days will be harder than others. The important part is showing up for yourself more often than not. Each little checkmark is a step toward your dreams and your growth. Keep going—you're doing great.

VI
Learning from Failures

6.1 Changing Your Perspective on Failure

Failure. It's a word loaded with emotion — disappointment, shame, guilt, sadness. But here's the thing no one told us when we were growing up:

? Failure is a part of success, not the opposite of it.

?? When Everything Feels Like It's Falling Apart...

Let's be honest. When you fail, it doesn't just hurt your mind — it hurts your soul. It makes you question everything:

"Am I even good enough?"

"Did I waste all this time for nothing?"

"What will people think of me?"

It's easy to spiral down that road. But pause for a second and ask yourself:

? What if this moment — this exact failure — is the turning point of your story?

Do you really think that every successful person walked on a smooth road? No potholes? No dead ends? No detours?

That's not how real life works.
The truth is: every great success story begins with failure. Not one. Not two. But often many.

? Failure Isn't a Full Stop — It's a Comma.

It's not the end of the sentence; it's just a pause. Something to make you pause and rethink. A moment to catch your breath and reflect.

Let me give you a raw example:
Have you ever tried so hard at something — studied for weeks, prepared for a speech, practiced for hours — only to still fall short?

You probably felt crushed. Unseen. Not good enough.

But later — days, months, or even years — you realized something.

You didn't fail because you were weak.

You failed because you were still growing.

That failure became fuel.

It taught you patience, resilience, humility.

It made you hungry to rise, stronger to restart.

? You Are Not the Failure.

You are not defined by your lowest moment.

Let me say that again, because I want you to feel it:

? You are not your failure. You are who you choose to become after it.

That's what truly matters. The failure might have knocked you down, but what makes you unbreakable is your decision to rise again — bruised, wiser, and more determined.

? Reframe the Mindset

Let's flip some common negative thoughts about failure into powerful beliefs:

Limiting Thought

Empowering Reframe

"I'm not good enough."

"I'm still learning, and that's okay."

"I failed, so I'll never succeed."

"Failure is part of the journey — not the end."

"People will judge me."

"People who truly care will support me, not shame me."

"I wasted my time."

"I gained experience that no book could teach."

♥? A Letter to You, From Someone Who's Been There

Dear You,

You are not behind.

You are not a disappointment.

You are becoming — and that's a beautiful, messy, brave thing.

You might be tired. Confused. Doubting your path.

But just keep showing up. That's enough for now.

You don't need to have all the answers.

You just need the courage to try again.

Because one day, you'll look back and say,

"I didn't give up on myself. And that made all the difference."

With love and belief,
Someone who understands

6.2 Stories of Famous Failures and Successes

Sometimes, we need more than just motivational words — we need proof. Real-life stories of people who fell down, got laughed at, faced rejection, and still rose beyond belief.

These stories aren't here to impress you — they're here to remind you that you're not alone in your journey. If they can rise, you can too.

? J.K. Rowling — From Rejected to Revered

Before Harry Potter became a global phenomenon, J.K. Rowling was:

A struggling single mother on welfare,

Battling depression,

Rejected by 12 publishers.

She could've given up. She could've said, "Maybe I'm not good enough." But she didn't. She kept going.

Her manuscript was finally accepted by a small publishing house — and the rest is history. Today, she's one of the most successful authors in the world.

But behind her fame is a story of deep failure, persistence, and courage.

? Thomas Edison — "I Found 10,000 Ways That Didn't Work"

Before Edison invented the lightbulb, he failed at it over 1,000 times. Can you imagine how many people mocked him?

But instead of calling those failures, he said:

"I have not failed. I've just found 10,000 ways that won't work."

That mindset changed history.

? Oprah Winfrey — "You're Not Fit for Television"

Before she became the queen of talk shows, Oprah was fired from her first TV job because she was "too emotional" and "unfit for television."

Imagine being told your deepest strength is your weakness?

But she owned her story. She used her empathy, her vulnerability, and her voice to become one of the most influential women on the planet.

? Michael Jordan — Cut from His High School Team

Yes, the Michael Jordan — the basketball legend — was cut from his high school team because his coach didn't think he was good enough.

Instead of quitting, he practiced harder, longer, with more fire in his heart.

Later, he said:

"I've missed more than 9,000 shots. I've lost almost 300 games. I've failed over and over again — and that is why I succeed."

? Amitabh Bachchan — Rejected by All India Radio

Amitabh's deep baritone voice, which is now iconic, was once the reason he was rejected. All India Radio told him his voice wasn't suitable for radio.

He went on to become one of the greatest actors in Indian cinema, loved for the same voice he was once told was a flaw.

? So, What's the Common Thread?

Every one of these people:

Faced rejection,

Was told "you can't,"

Failed publicly,

Felt crushed.

But they all had one thing in common:

They didn't let failure define their worth.

They allowed it to refine their strength.

And you?

You have that same power within you. Maybe you don't see it yet, but it's there — waiting to rise from the ashes of your setbacks.

? Your Turn

Take a breath.

Think about someone you admire — someone you look up to.

Now, go Google their journey.

Chances are, you'll find pain, rejection, failure — just like yours.

Because success doesn't come in a straight line.

It comes in loops, curves, detours, and breakdowns.

You're not falling behind.

You're in the making.

6.3 Extracting Lessons from Failure

Failure.

Even the word can sting.

We've all felt it — that heavy pit in the stomach, the embarrassment, the shame, the whisper in your mind saying, "You're not good enough."

But what if we changed the way we looked at failure?

What if... instead of seeing it as a punishment, we saw it as a teacher?

? What Is Failure Trying to Teach You?

Behind every failed attempt is a message.

Sometimes it's about your strategy.

Sometimes it's about your timing.

And sometimes — it's about your inner growth.

Think of failure as a mirror.

It reflects:

What didn't work,

What you could do differently,

What you need to learn next.

Not to break your spirit — but to sharpen your vision.

? Reflection Prompts That Help You Learn from Failure

Let's pause for a moment.

Think about a recent failure — personal, academic, professional, emotional, anything.

Ask yourself:

What actually went wrong?

Be honest, not judgmental. Maybe it was a lack of planning, preparation, communication?

What part of this was in your control?

We often blame ourselves for things we never controlled. Separate the two.

What did you discover about yourself in this process?

Maybe you found you're more resilient than you thought. Or maybe you need better boundaries.

What can you try differently next time?

Every failure leaves behind clues — if you're willing to listen.

? Growth Isn't Always Loud

We celebrate success loudly.

But growth — true growth — happens in silence:

When you cry and still wake up to try again.

When you admit your mistake and learn from it.

When you fail but refuse to give up.

Those moments build your character.

That's the foundation for a future that's not just successful — but deeply authentic.

❤?? You're Not Defined by Failure

You're not your mistakes.

You're not your failed relationships.

You're not the exam you didn't pass.

You're not the business idea that didn't work out.

You are:

A work in progress,
A learner,
A fighter.
And every time you reflect, adjust, and move forward — you grow closer to your highest self.
So take the lesson.
Write it down.
Own it.
Then let the failure go.
You are not your past — you are your possibility.
6.4 Failure Reflection Worksheet
Let's pause.
This is your moment of stillness — to sit with what hurt, learn from it, and gently move forward.
You don't need to judge yourself here.
You just need to be honest with yourself.
Take a notebook, or print this out if you'd like, and answer these prompts slowly and truthfully.
? Part 1: Describe the Failure
What happened?
(Write the incident/situation in detail)
→
How did it make you feel?
(List all emotions — sadness, anger, guilt, numbness, confusion, etc.)
→
What expectations did you have that were not met?
→

? Part 2: Analyze the Experience
What part of this failure was in your control?
→

What was out of your control?
→

Did you prepare or plan enough for this?
→

Were there any signs that things might go wrong — that you ignored?
→

? Part 3: Extract the Lessons

What did this experience teach you about:
Yourself?
→

Other people?
→

Life?
→

If you could go back and do it differently, what would you change?
→

What is the one key lesson you will carry forward from this failure?
→

? Part 4: Moving Forward
What's your next step after this failure?
(Be specific — restart? replan? upskill? heal?)
→

What support or help do you need right now?
(Could be a mentor, friend, coach, rest, therapy, course, etc.)
→

Write an affirmation that reminds you this failure does not define you.
(Example: "I am learning, not losing.")
→

? Final Note:
Keep this worksheet.
Revisit it when you feel low again.
Let it remind you:
You faced it.
You reflected.
You grew.
And you are stronger because of it.
6.2 Using Strengths to Your Advantage
You've probably been told what you're not good at far more often than what you are good at.
It's how most of us grow up — corrected, compared, constantly measured.
And somewhere along the way, your real strengths got buried under expectations, doubt, and fear.
But listen carefully:
You already have everything inside you to build the life you want.

Yes, you.

Not when you become "more confident" or "more educated" or "more perfect."

Right now. As you are.

? Reconnecting With Your Inner Power

Think back to moments when you felt alive —

Maybe when you helped a friend through pain.

Or when you organized something beautifully.

Or when you stood up for someone, or shared your truth.

Those moments weren't just coincidences.

They were glimpses of your strength in action.

You didn't need applause.

You didn't wait for permission.

You just showed up — and that is where your power lies.

? Let Go of the "Not Enough" Story

You're not "too quiet" — you're reflective.

You're not "too emotional" — you feel deeply.

You're not "too intense" — you care.

What people criticize in you might actually be your greatest asset.

If you've ever felt like you don't fit in —

maybe it's because you were born to stand out.

So stop editing yourself.

Stop waiting to be accepted to be worthy.

Start using those strengths unapologetically.

? Turn Strength Into Action

Here's a mindset shift you need:

"My strength is not just for me. It's for the world."

Ask yourself:

How can I bring this strength into my daily actions?

Can I use my creativity to solve a problem at work or school?

Can I use my kindness to build better relationships?

Can I use my resilience to inspire someone who's breaking?

Your strength becomes powerful when you use it with purpose.

✍? Journal Prompt

Write down your top 3 strengths (you can use the list from the previous section).

For each one, answer these:

How have I used this strength in the past?

How can I use it more intentionally now?

Who can benefit from this strength today?

❤? From Me to You

Dear reader,

You are not here by accident.

Your pain has shaped you.

Your strength is not an add-on — it's part of your survival.

So the next time you doubt yourself, remember:

Even when you didn't believe in yourself —

your strength carried you here.

Now, it's time you carry it forward.

Use it. Own it. Let the world feel it.

7.3 Building Confidence Through Strengths (Extended)

Let's get real:

Confidence doesn't magically appear one morning when you wake up.

It's not gifted. It's built — slowly, intentionally, and patiently.

And here's the most beautiful part —

You don't need to wait until you "fix" yourself to start feeling confident.

You just need to start noticing what's already right about you.

? Confidence Isn't Loud — It's Real

We've been made to believe that confidence looks like walking into a room and owning it.

And sure, sometimes it does.

But more often, confidence is quieter.

It's choosing to show up even when you're nervous.

It's sending that email you're scared to send.

It's speaking your truth even if your voice shakes.

Confidence is saying:

"I know I'm not perfect — and I still choose myself."

? Strengths: Your Foundation of Confidence

When you build your confidence from your strengths, you stop chasing external validation.

Let's take some examples:

If you're a good listener — your strength brings people comfort. That's powerful.

If you're great at organizing — your strength creates clarity and order in chaos.

If you're full of empathy — your strength brings healing and support.

When you recognize how your natural gifts make a difference, you stop trying to be someone else. You start trusting who you already are.

? Confidence Grows with Evidence

Here's a simple truth:

Confidence grows when you collect proof of your capabilities.

Every time you:

Solve a problem

Help someone

Speak up in a tough moment

Try something new

...you are gathering evidence that you're capable.

So don't dismiss the small wins. They are the building blocks of your self-belief.

Celebrate the micro-victories. That's where big confidence is born.

✍? Exercise: Strength-Based Confidence Log

Let's make this real.

Step 1: Choose one of your core strengths.

Step 2: Write down 3 situations from the last month where you used it.

Step 3: Reflect: How did using this strength make you feel? What was the impact?

You'll be surprised how often you've already been standing in your power — without even realizing it.

? A Note From Me to You

You don't need to wait for the world to clap before you feel good about yourself.

You don't need a spotlight to shine.

Your confidence doesn't begin outside — it starts within, by trusting your strength, even when no one's watching.

So if you're walking a path that feels lonely, remember:

You're not behind. You're just on your own timeline.

And that's more than okay. That's extraordinary.

7.4 Strengths Inventory Exercise

It's easy to get caught up in what we're not good at.

We beat ourselves up for the mistakes, compare ourselves to others, and start believing we're not enough.

But here's something nobody tells you often enough:

You have strengths that the world needs — even if you don't fully see them yet.

Let's change that today.

? What is a Strengths Inventory?

Think of it as your personal treasure map.

A Strengths Inventory is a mindful exercise where you stop and reflect on:

What you naturally do well

What people often thank you for

What energizes you

What feels meaningful when you do it

It's not just about big skills like public speaking or leadership. It's also about the small, quiet gifts — patience, compassion, being trustworthy, showing up.

This is your moment to stop minimizing your magic.

?? Exercise: Discovering Your Inner Strengths

Take out your journal, open a blank page, and write across the top:

"Who am I when I'm at my best?"

Now answer these prompts:

? Prompt 1: What activities make me feel alive and purposeful?

Think of moments where time flew because you were so absorbed.

Maybe it was helping a friend, solving a problem, writing, creating, or teaching.

? Prompt 2: What do people appreciate about me?

What compliments do you often receive?

What do people come to you for help with?

Don't brush them off as "nothing." These are signs of your strength.

? Prompt 3: What have I overcome that made me stronger?

Your resilience is a strength. Your ability to heal is a strength.

Every challenge you've moved through is proof of your inner power.

? Mirror Statement: Claim Your Strength

Stand in front of the mirror. Look into your eyes — not past them. Say this:

"I am strong because I've survived.

I am powerful because I care.

I am enough — just as I am."

Do it every day for 7 days. Speak to yourself with the love and belief you deserve.

? Reminder for You

You don't need to become someone else to be strong.
You need to become more of who you already are.
Your strengths aren't always loud or flashy.
Sometimes, strength is quiet courage, soft kindness, and fierce honesty.
And that's more than enough.

VII

From Confusion to Clarity

8.1 The Transformation Process (Extended)

Have you ever walked through a thick fog — the kind where you can't even see two steps ahead?

That's what confusion feels like in life.

You try to make sense of things, but everything is blurry. Emotions overwhelm you. People's voices mix with your own doubts. You feel lost, tired, unsure.

But here's the good news:

Clarity is not a lightning bolt. It's a slow sunrise.

? How Transformation Begins

Clarity doesn't come from one magical moment.

It begins when you choose to stop fighting the confusion and start listening to what it's trying to teach you.

Transformation happens when:

You pause instead of panicking.

You reflect instead of rushing.

You begin to trust that even in this messy middle, you're growing.

"It's okay if you don't have it all figured out. The fog doesn't mean you're failing — it means you're learning."

? Step-by-Step Shift from Confusion to Clarity

Let's break down the transformation:

Step 1: Acceptance

Stop running from your confusion. It's a part of your journey, not a flaw in it.

Tell yourself:

"I may not know where I'm going, but I trust that this phase has a purpose."

Step 2: Self-Awareness

Begin identifying what exactly feels unclear. Is it your purpose? A relationship? A career decision?

Name it. Because you can't solve what you don't understand.

Step 3: Honest Reflection

Look within without fear. Ask yourself:

What do I truly want?

What have I been avoiding?

What belief is keeping me stuck?

Step 4: Small, Aligned Action

Clarity doesn't come from overthinking — it comes from moving.

Take one step, no matter how small, toward what feels right. Clarity follows courage.

? A Soft Reminder

If your heart is heavy with confusion today, know this:

You're not broken. You're blooming.

Confusion is often the sign that you're evolving — shedding old layers to make space for new growth.

So don't rush your clarity.

Let it come like morning light — gently, steadily, and always right on time.

8.2 Signs You Are Gaining Clarity (Extended)

Do you ever wonder, "Am I even making progress?"

Sometimes clarity sneaks in so gently that we don't even realize we're stepping out of the fog. But if you pause, breathe, and look around — you'll see the signs.

Because slowly, something starts to change.

? The Subtle Signs of Clarity

1. You Begin to Trust Yourself Again

That voice inside you — the one that's been quiet, second-guessing, afraid — it starts to speak up with calmness. You begin to feel like you again. You may not have all the answers, but you trust that you can handle whatever comes.

"I don't know everything yet, but I know myself better now."

2. You Stop Chasing, Start Choosing

Instead of rushing to please everyone, you're learning to pause and ask: "Does this align with who I am?"

You're not driven by desperation anymore — you're led by intention.

3. You Feel Lighter

Not every day is perfect, but you're not carrying as much emotional weight.

You begin letting go — of people, beliefs, or habits that no longer feel right. It hurts, but it also sets you free.

4. Your Priorities Become Clear

You notice what truly matters. Your time, energy, and focus start flowing toward what brings peace — not just what brings approval.

5. You Start Taking Authentic Action

You're no longer paralyzed.

You make that phone call. Write that journal entry. Join that class. Say "no" without guilt. Say "yes" to things that scare you but feel right.

That, my friend, is clarity in motion.

❤? Talk with the Reader

Let me tell you something that might surprise you...

You don't need to be 100% clear to move forward.

Even 10% clarity is enough to take one honest step.

Clarity is not perfection. It's progress.

It's that peaceful moment when, after days of emotional noise, your heart whispers:

"This... this feels right."

And if you've heard that whisper, even once —

You're already on your way.

8.3 Creating Your Vision for the Future (Extended)

Close your eyes for a moment. Take a deep breath.

Now imagine a life where you wake up feeling aligned — not rushed, not lost, not confused. A life where your choices reflect your truth. Your relationships feel safe. Your work has meaning. Your days are filled with more peace than pressure.

That life? It's not a fantasy. It starts with a vision.

? Why You Need a Vision

When you're walking through confusion, having a vision is like spotting a lighthouse in the fog. You may still feel lost at sea, but now you have something to sail toward. A direction. A pull.

And no — it doesn't have to be perfectly clear right away. Your vision can be messy, evolving, even blurred at the edges. What matters is that it's yours.

? Steps to Crafting Your Vision

1. Ask Yourself the Right Questions

Let your heart speak. Journal answers to questions like:

What does a peaceful day look like for me?

Who am I when I feel most alive?

What do I want more of in life?

What kind of relationships do I deserve?

How do I want to show up in the world?

These questions aren't just for dreaming — they help you return to yourself.

2. Picture It with Detail

Don't just say "I want success."

Visualize it:

What does success look like in your life?

Where are you? Who are you with? How do you feel?

What are you doing that brings you fulfillment?

Make your vision so real in your mind that it begins to feel like a memory from the future.

3. Choose Three Core Feelings

What emotions do you want your life to be rooted in?

Peace? Passion? Freedom? Connection? Impact?

Let these be your compass when making decisions.

? Talk with the Reader

Let me gently remind you:

You don't have to chase someone else's dream.

You're allowed to create your own version of success.

You're allowed to grow at your own pace.

You're allowed to rewrite your story as many times as you need to.

So take that pen.

Take that vision.

And begin sketching the life you deserve — not later, not someday — but now.

8.4 Vision Board or Visualization Exercise (Extended)

You've now tapped into your dreams. You've felt them, seen them in your mind, and maybe even written them down. But how do you bring them closer to reality?

That's where visualization and vision boards come in — tools that turn your inner world into a powerful guide for your outer journey.

? What is a Vision Board?

A vision board is a visual representation of the life you desire — using images, words, and symbols that align with your goals, values, and emotions.

It's not just a craft project. It's a way to anchor your intentions and remind yourself of what truly matters — especially on the tough days.

When you SEE your goals daily, they stop being just ideas. They start becoming promises.

? Why Visualization Works

Visualization is a mental rehearsal. Top athletes do it. Speakers do it. Leaders do it.

Because when you visualize yourself achieving something, your brain starts building new neural pathways — preparing your body and mind to believe, act, and receive.

You're literally rewiring yourself to succeed.

?? How to Create Your Vision Board

Materials You'll Need:

Old magazines, newspapers, or printed images

A notebook, chart paper, or canvas

Glue, scissors, stickers, or digital design tools (like Canva or Pinterest)

Steps:

Set the vibe. Light a candle, play music, or sit somewhere quiet. Breathe in deeply. Connect with your heart.

Choose your themes. Career? Self-love? Confidence? Health? Relationships? Pick a few key life areas.

Find your visuals. Cut or save pictures that feel right. Trust your gut. Look for images, quotes, symbols, and colors that energize you.

Assemble with intention. Place your visuals creatively. Let it reflect YOU — not perfection, but purpose.

Keep it visible. Place it somewhere you'll see it daily — your wall, journal, wardrobe, or phone background.

? Bonus: Guided Visualization Exercise

Close your eyes again. Just for a minute.

Imagine waking up in your dream life.
You feel calm, fulfilled, excited.
You stretch, and smile — because your life feels right.

Who are you becoming? What are you doing?

Sit with this version of yourself. Say hello.

Visualize this daily. It's not magic — it's mindset work.

? Talk With the Reader

This is your life to design.

Not your parents'. Not society's. Not someone else's idea of "perfect."

You don't need to have it all figured out. You just need the courage to begin visualizing. Once you see it, you'll start believing it. And when you believe it, you'll build it.

So dream with your eyes open.

VIII
Letting Go of What Hurts

9.1 What Are Healthy Boundaries?

Boundaries are like invisible fences that protect your emotional, mental, and physical space. They define what you are comfortable with and how you want to be treated by others. Healthy boundaries are essential because they help you maintain respect for yourself and ensure that others respect you too.

Think of boundaries as the personal rules you set in your life — they tell people how close they can get, what they can say, and how they can behave around you. Without these boundaries, it's easy to feel overwhelmed, taken advantage of, or drained by the people around you.

Healthy boundaries don't mean shutting people out or being harsh. They mean understanding your limits and calmly communicating them. For example, if you need time alone after a long day, it's okay to say, "I need some quiet time right now." If someone is asking too much of your time or energy, you have every right to say no.

Many times, especially for youth and women, setting boundaries feels difficult. Maybe you were taught to always please others, or you fear losing relationships if you say no. But the truth is, boundaries are a form of self-love and respect. They create the space you need to grow, recharge, and be your best self.

Healthy boundaries also teach others how to treat you. When you communicate your limits clearly and kindly, people learn to respect your needs, making your relationships healthier and more balanced. It's not about building walls but about creating safe spaces for yourself and others.

Remember, boundaries are not fixed. They can change as you grow, learn, and understand yourself better. What felt right for you last year may feel different today, and that's okay. The important thing is to keep checking in with yourself and honor what feels right for you at any moment.

9.2 Why We Struggle to Say No

Saying "no" seems simple, right? But for many of us, especially youth and women, it's one of the hardest words to say. Why is that?

First, saying no often feels like we might hurt someone's feelings. We worry about disappointing others or making them angry. We don't want to come off as rude or selfish. So instead, we say yes even when our heart screams no.

Second, there's fear—fear of rejection or being left out. We want to belong, to be accepted. Saying no feels like we're risking that connection, so we keep agreeing, even if it drains us.

Third, many of us have been raised to put others first, to be "good," "helpful," and "obedient." Saying no sometimes feels like breaking those learned rules. It can make us feel guilty or selfish, even when setting boundaries is exactly what we need.

Fourth, sometimes we don't even realize we need to say no because we haven't fully identified our own limits. Without knowing what we can or cannot handle, it becomes harder to refuse requests.

But here's the truth: Saying no is not rude or selfish. It is an act of self-care. Every time you say no to something that doesn't serve you, you say yes to your well-being and peace of mind.

Learning to say no is a skill. It takes practice, patience, and kindness toward yourself. The more you practice, the more confident you become in honoring your own needs without guilt.

Remember, you deserve respect, and respecting your own limits is the first step in teaching others how to respect you.

9.3 Steps to Assertive Communication

Assertive communication is about expressing your thoughts, feelings, and needs openly and honestly while respecting others. It's the sweet spot between being passive (not speaking up) and aggressive (being forceful or disrespectful). Learning to communicate assertively is a powerful tool, especially when setting boundaries and saying no.

Here are simple steps to help you communicate assertively:

1. Know Your Feelings and Needs

Before you speak up, take a moment to understand what you want and how you feel. Are you uncomfortable? Overwhelmed? Do you need time or space? When you know your feelings clearly, it's easier to express them calmly.

2. Use "I" Statements

Start your sentences with "I" instead of "You." For example, say "I feel overwhelmed when I have too many commitments," instead of "You always ask too much of me." This approach keeps the focus on your experience and reduces blame or conflict.

3. Be Clear and Direct

Say what you mean in a straightforward way. Avoid beating around the bush or expecting others to read your mind. For example, "I can't take on this task right now" is clearer than "I'm not sure if I can."

4. Maintain Calm Body Language

Your tone, facial expressions, and posture matter. Keep your voice steady and calm, maintain eye contact, and stand or sit in a relaxed but confident posture. This shows you mean what you say and respect yourself.

5. Practice Saying No Gracefully

Saying no doesn't have to be harsh. You can be polite but firm. For example, "Thank you for thinking of me, but I won't be able to help this time." If needed, offer an alternative or a future possibility, but don't feel pressured to explain excessively.

6. Prepare for Pushback

Sometimes people will try to convince you or react negatively. Stay firm and repeat your boundary if needed, calmly and without guilt. Remember, your well-being is important.

7. Practice Regularly

Like any skill, assertive communication gets easier with practice. Start small — say no to minor requests and gradually build your confidence for bigger situations.

Remember: Being assertive is a way to honor your feelings and needs while maintaining respect for others. It is not about winning or controlling; it's about honest and respectful dialogue.

9.4 Personal Boundaries Practice Sheet

Setting personal boundaries can feel unfamiliar or even uncomfortable at first, but practicing helps build confidence and clarity about what you will and won't accept in your relationships and daily life. Use this practice sheet as a guide to explore and strengthen your boundaries.

Step 1: Identify Your Boundaries

Think about different areas of your life where boundaries matter. Write down your thoughts:

Emotional Boundaries: How much emotional energy can you give without feeling drained?

Physical Boundaries: What kind of physical contact or personal space feels comfortable?

Time Boundaries: How much time are you willing to dedicate to others versus yourself?

Mental Boundaries: What kinds of opinions or beliefs are okay for you to hear or tolerate?

Material Boundaries: What are your limits about sharing possessions or money?

Step 2: Recognize Boundary Violations

List recent situations where you felt uncomfortable, overwhelmed, or resentful. Ask yourself:

What boundary was crossed?

How did it make you feel?

Did you communicate your feelings or needs?

Step 3: Practice Assertive Responses

Write down how you can respond assertively in similar situations in the future. For example:

"I need some time to think about this before I give an answer."

"I feel uncomfortable when you speak to me that way. Please stop."

"I appreciate your offer, but I have to say no this time."

Step 4: Self-Check and Reflection

After practicing boundaries, reflect on your experience:

How did it feel to speak up?

What challenges did you face?

What positive changes did you notice?

Step 5: Set a Small Boundary Goal

Choose one area to focus on this week. For example:

Saying no to an extra task at work.

Asking for personal space with a family member.

Limiting time spent on social media to protect your mental health.

Remember:

Boundaries are about protecting your well-being and creating healthier relationships. It's okay to start small, and it's okay to adjust as you grow.

Practice kindness with yourself along the way.

IX

Building Emotional Resilience

10.1 What is Resilience?

Resilience is one of those invisible powers we all have inside us — even when it feels like we don't. It's not about never falling or never feeling overwhelmed. It's about how we rise after we've been knocked down. Life is unpredictable, and challenges come to all of us, especially to young people and women who often carry the weight of expectations, responsibilities, and sometimes even unfair judgments. Resilience is what keeps us moving forward despite all of that.

Imagine resilience as an emotional muscle. Just like your body gets stronger when you exercise, your ability to bounce back and heal grows stronger when you face adversity and learn from it. It's okay to feel hurt, scared, or lost — those feelings don't mean you're weak. In fact, they mean you're human. Resilience allows you to honor those feelings without letting them define you.

Building resilience means learning to be patient with yourself when things don't go as planned. It means giving yourself the grace to say, "I'm struggling, but I will keep trying." It means understanding that setbacks and failures are not the end of your story; they are part of the journey that shapes your growth.

For many women and youth, resilience also means breaking through societal pressures to "be strong" all the time, to hide vulnerabilities, or to put others' needs before their own. Real strength comes from embracing your

• 56 •

whole self — the good days and the bad — and trusting that you have the power to heal, learn, and keep going.

Most importantly, resilience is not a solo journey. It's okay to ask for help, lean on friends, family, mentors, or professionals. Being resilient doesn't mean carrying the world on your shoulders alone; it means knowing when to reach out and allowing others to support you as you rebuild.

When you nurture resilience, you're planting seeds of hope, courage, and determination within yourself. These seeds will help you grow into a stronger, wiser, and more compassionate person who can face life's storms with confidence and heart.

10.2 Tools to Strengthen Emotional Flexibility

Emotional flexibility is the ability to adapt your feelings and reactions to whatever life throws at you. It's like having a mental toolbox filled with different tools to help you cope, recover, and keep moving forward, no matter how tough things get. When you're emotionally flexible, you don't get stuck in one way of thinking or feeling—you allow yourself to experience emotions fully but don't let them control your entire world.

So, how can you build this emotional flexibility? Here are some simple yet powerful tools you can start using today:

1. Mindful Awareness

Being mindful means paying attention to your thoughts and feelings without judgment. Instead of pushing away sadness, anger, or fear, you notice them and accept that they are part of your current experience. This doesn't mean you have to like those feelings; it just means you're giving yourself permission to feel. Mindfulness creates space for healing because you stop fighting yourself.

2. Deep Breathing and Grounding Techniques

When emotions get intense, our body reacts—heart races, breath quickens, mind spins. Deep breathing slows all that down. Try breathing in slowly for four counts, holding for four, then breathing out for six. Repeat this until you feel calmer. Grounding exercises, like focusing on the feel of your feet on the floor or the texture of an object in your hand, help bring you back to the present moment when emotions feel overwhelming.

3. Journaling Your Feelings

Writing down what you feel, without censoring yourself, is a powerful way to release pent-up emotions. Don't worry about grammar or style—just let the words flow. You may be surprised how writing can bring clarity, perspective, and relief.

4. Positive Self-Talk and Affirmations

Often, our harshest critic lives inside our own minds. When you catch yourself thinking, "I'm not good enough," pause and replace that thought with something kinder like, "I am doing my best, and that's enough." Affirmations are positive statements you repeat to yourself to build confidence and calm your inner voice.

5. Seeking Support

Remember, emotional flexibility doesn't mean doing it all alone. Talk to someone you trust—a friend, family member, or counselor. Sharing your feelings can lighten your burden and sometimes give you new ways to look at things.

6. Allowing Yourself Time to Heal

Emotions can't be rushed. Sometimes you need days, weeks, or even months to process a tough experience. Give yourself permission to take the time you need without guilt or pressure.

By practicing these tools regularly, you develop the strength to face your emotions without fear. You learn that it's okay to feel deeply, yet still keep moving forward. Emotional flexibility is a skill, and like any skill, it grows stronger the more you practice it.

You might not be able to control what happens around you, but you can control how you respond. And that is where true power lies.

10.3 Real-life Stories of Resilient Women and Youth

Sometimes, when life feels overwhelming and you're drowning in your struggles, hearing about others who have faced similar battles and come out stronger can be like a lifeline. These stories are not just inspirational—they are proof that resilience is real and possible for everyone, including you.

Meet Aisha, a young woman from a small town who dreamed of becoming a teacher. Her family didn't support her education, and many told her she should focus on marriage instead. Aisha faced rejection and loneliness but never gave up. She worked odd jobs, studied at night, and kept reminding herself of her dream. Today, Aisha teaches hundreds of children and runs a small community library. Her journey wasn't easy, but every challenge built her inner strength.

Then there's Raj, a young man who grew up in poverty and lost his father early. The weight of responsibility was heavy, and confusion about his future clouded his mind. Yet Raj learned to ask for help and found mentors who believed in him. Through sheer determination, he secured a scholarship to study engineering and now mentors youth from similar backgrounds, showing them the path forward.

These stories teach us that resilience is not about never falling; it's about rising each time we fall. It's about holding on to hope even when everything seems lost. It's about finding light in the darkest moments.

You might not be Aisha or Raj, but your story is just as important. Your struggles, your tears, your small victories—they all build your resilience every day. Keep going, because the world needs your strength and your voice.

10.4 Daily Resilience Builder Task

Building resilience is not a one-time event; it's a daily practice. Think of it as exercising your emotional muscles—each day you do a little, you become stronger, more flexible, and better prepared to handle life's challenges. Here's a simple yet powerful daily task to help you build your resilience:

1. Start Your Day with a Positive Intention

Before you get out of bed, take a moment to set an intention for the day. It could be as simple as "I will be kind to myself today," or "I will face challenges with courage." This small act shifts your mindset and prepares you to face the day with strength.

2. Practice Gratitude

Write down three things you are grateful for every day. Gratitude doesn't ignore the struggles—it simply reminds you that there are still good things, no matter how small. This practice rewires your brain to focus on hope and abundance.

3. Take Care of Your Body

Resilience is not just mental or emotional; it's physical too. Drink water, eat nourishing food, and move your body—even a short walk or gentle stretch helps. When your body feels cared for, your mind and emotions follow.

4. Challenge One Negative Thought

When you notice a negative thought creeping in, pause and ask yourself: "Is this thought really true? Is there another way to see this?" Replacing negative thoughts with kinder, more realistic ones is a key to emotional strength.

5. Reflect Before Bed

Before sleeping, spend five minutes reflecting on your day. Celebrate your wins, no matter how small. Acknowledge your struggles without judgment. This reflection helps you see your growth and prepares your mind for rest and renewal.

Try to do this task every day for a week and notice how your ability to handle stress and setbacks improves. Remember, resilience is a journey, not a destination. Each small step counts, and you're not alone in this process.

Breaking the Myth of Perfection

Perfection — it's a word that sounds beautiful but often feels like a heavy chain holding us back. Many of us grow up believing that we must be perfect in everything: our studies, our work, our relationships, even how we look or behave. But here's the truth nobody tells us enough — perfection is a myth. It's an impossible standard that no one can reach, yet it keeps us trapped in endless self-judgment and fear.

Trying to be perfect all the time drains your energy and steals your joy. When you're chasing perfection, mistakes feel like failures instead of lessons. You stop trying new things because you're scared of not being flawless. You compare yourself to others and feel like you don't measure up. And worse, you forget that being human means being beautifully imperfect.

Breaking free from the myth of perfection starts with self-compassion. Give yourself permission to be human — to make mistakes, to have bad days, to be enough just as you are. Remember, growth happens in the messiness of life, not in perfect moments. Some of the strongest, most inspiring people you admire have failed, stumbled, and risen again many times.

This chapter will help you let go of perfectionism and embrace your authentic self — flaws, scars, and all. Because real success is not about being perfect, it's about being brave enough to keep moving forward, no matter what.

11.2 Reframing the Meaning of Success

What does success mean to you? Is it climbing the career ladder, earning a big salary, or getting everyone's approval? Society often paints success with a narrow brush — as if it's only about titles, money, or external achievements. But true success is so much deeper and more personal than that.

Success is about finding fulfillment and peace in your journey, not just reaching a destination. It means living in alignment with your values, being true to yourself, and growing every day. It's waking up with purpose and going to bed feeling you gave your best, even if things didn't turn out perfectly.

When you reframe success this way, you release yourself from the pressure of constant comparison and perfection. You start to celebrate small wins, like learning something new, overcoming a fear, or simply showing up for yourself. Success becomes a series of meaningful moments, not just milestones on a checklist.

This shift changes how you view setbacks too. Instead of failures, they become opportunities to learn and pivot. You become more resilient, more patient, and kinder to yourself. Success stops being about impressing others and starts being about honoring your own growth and happiness.

In this chapter, you'll explore what success truly means to you and learn practical ways to create your own definition — one that empowers and inspires you to keep moving forward with confidence.

11.3 Personal Success Definition Worksheet

Success looks different for everyone. This worksheet is designed to help you discover what success really means to you — beyond what others expect or society dictates. Take your time with these questions. Be honest, open, and kind to yourself.

1. Reflect on your past achievements.

What moments in your life have made you feel proud or fulfilled?

Why did these moments matter to you?

2. Identify your core values.

What values are non-negotiable for you? (Examples: honesty, creativity, freedom, family)

How do these values influence your decisions and goals?

3. Imagine your ideal life.

What does a 'successful day' look like for you?

How do you feel physically, emotionally, and mentally?

Who are you with? What are you doing?

4. Define success in your own words.

Write a personal success statement that inspires you.

Example: "Success for me means living with integrity, learning every day, and nurturing meaningful relationships."

5. Set success goals.

What are three goals that align with your definition of success?

How will you measure progress toward these goals?

6. Identify potential challenges.

What might get in the way of your success?

How can you prepare to face these challenges?

7. Affirm your journey.

Write a positive affirmation to remind yourself why your definition of success matters.

Remember: There is no right or wrong answer here. This worksheet is your personal map — one that will guide you toward a success that feels authentic and fulfilling.

12.1 Accepting the Past

Accepting the past is one of the hardest but most freeing steps on your journey. It doesn't mean forgetting or pretending bad things didn't happen. Instead, it means making peace with what has shaped you, without letting it define or limit your future.

Our past experiences—good and bad—are like chapters in a book. Some chapters are joyful and uplifting, others painful and confusing. But every chapter adds to the story of you. Accepting the past means embracing your whole story, with compassion and understanding.

Often, we hold onto pain because we fear letting go means losing a part of ourselves. But clinging to past hurt only keeps us stuck in old patterns and emotions. It's okay to acknowledge the pain, but it's equally important to choose healing.

How to start accepting your past:

Acknowledge your feelings. Don't rush yourself or suppress emotions. Cry, journal, talk to someone you trust—whatever helps you process.

Shift your perspective. Try to see your past as a teacher, not a jailer. What lessons has it offered? What strengths have you gained?

Practice forgiveness. Forgiveness isn't about excusing what happened; it's about freeing yourself from bitterness. This may be forgiving others or even forgiving yourself.

Be patient with yourself. Acceptance is a process, not a one-time event. Some days will feel easier, others harder—and that's okay.

Remember, your past shapes you but does not control your future. Accepting it allows you to reclaim your power, grow stronger, and create a life that feels whole and free.

12.2 Letting Go of Emotional Baggage

Emotional baggage is like carrying a heavy backpack filled with old hurts, regrets, fears, and unresolved feelings. It weighs you down, slows you, and often keeps you from moving forward in life. But here's the truth: you don't have to carry it forever.

Letting go of emotional baggage isn't about erasing memories or pretending everything was okay. It's about releasing the hold those emotions have on you so you can breathe easier, think clearer, and live more freely.

Why do we hold onto emotional baggage?

Fear of facing the pain or discomfort

Belief that holding onto anger or hurt protects us

Attachment to past identity or story

Uncertainty about who we are without those emotions

But holding on only keeps us stuck in the past. It affects our relationships, our confidence, and our ability to find peace. Letting go opens space for healing, growth, and new opportunities.

How to start letting go:

Identify what you're holding onto. Write down the feelings, memories, or people tied to your emotional weight.

Allow yourself to feel. Sometimes we avoid pain, but feeling it fully is the first step to release.

Practice self-compassion. Be gentle with yourself. Letting go takes time and courage.

Use rituals or symbolic acts. Some find writing letters they don't send, burning notes, or meditation helpful to mark the letting go process.

Seek support. Don't hesitate to reach out to trusted friends, mentors, or therapists for help.

Remember, letting go is not forgetting or giving up. It's reclaiming your energy and choosing peace. You deserve to travel light and walk your path with an open heart.

12.3 Healing Rituals and Habits

Healing isn't a one-time event; it's a daily practice. When you commit to small rituals and habits, you build a foundation that supports your emotional, mental, and even physical well-being. These rituals don't need to be complicated or time-consuming—they just need to be consistent and meaningful to you.

Why rituals and habits matter:

Rituals create a safe space to pause, reflect, and reconnect with yourself. They help you release stress, process emotions, and cultivate calm. Over time, they build resilience and a sense of control over your healing journey.

Simple healing rituals to try:

Morning mindfulness or meditation: Starting your day with a few moments of quiet focus can center your mind and set a positive tone.

Journaling: Write down your thoughts, feelings, and progress. Journaling helps you make sense of your emotions and track your healing.

Gratitude practice: Each day, note three things you are grateful for. Gratitude shifts your focus from what's wrong to what's right.

Movement: Whether it's yoga, walking, or dancing, moving your body helps release tension and boosts mood.

Breathing exercises: Deep, intentional breathing calms the nervous system and brings you back to the present moment.

Building new habits:

Healing also means replacing harmful patterns with nurturing ones. This might include setting boundaries, choosing positive company, or practicing self-kindness. Start small—pick one habit and focus on it for a few weeks before adding more.

Remember, healing is not linear. Some days will feel easier than others, and that's okay. The important part is showing up for yourself every day, with patience and love.

12.4 Emotional Cleanse Checklist

Emotional cleansing is like a detox for your heart and mind. Just as you cleanse your body to feel refreshed, you need to clear out emotional clutter that weighs you down. This checklist will help you create space inside yourself for peace, clarity, and growth.

Your Emotional Cleanse Checklist:

Identify Emotional Clutter:

Take time to notice what emotions you're holding onto that no longer serve you—resentment, guilt, anger, sadness. Write them down without judgment.

Allow Yourself to Feel:

Don't push away emotions. Let yourself experience them fully, even if they're painful. Suppressed feelings only grow louder inside.

Practice Forgiveness:

Forgiveness isn't about excusing hurtful actions but freeing yourself from the weight of anger or bitterness. Start by forgiving yourself, then others when you're ready.

Release Through Expression:

Cry, scream, write, or talk to someone you trust. Find healthy ways to express your feelings so they don't get bottled up.

Set Boundaries:

Protect your emotional space by saying no to toxic people or situations.

Boundaries are acts of self-respect and healing.

Engage in Soothing Activities:

Take baths, meditate, listen to calming music, or spend time in nature. These activities help your nervous system settle.

Practice Daily Affirmations:

Remind yourself of your worth, strength, and growth with positive statements. Replace self-criticism with kindness.

Limit Negative Inputs:

Reduce exposure to negative news, social media drama, or harmful conversations that drain your energy.

Create a Safe Space:

Dedicate a corner in your home for relaxation and reflection—fill it with things that bring comfort and joy.

Commit to Consistency:

Make emotional cleansing part of your routine. Healing is ongoing, and small daily steps build lasting change.

This checklist is a guide, not a strict rulebook. Adapt it to what feels right for you. The goal is to lighten your emotional load so you can step forward with clarity and peace.

X

Cultivating Self-Love.

13.1 What Self-Love Is and Isn't

Self-love is often misunderstood as arrogance or selfishness. But in truth, self-love is about respect, acceptance, and compassion towards oneself. It's recognizing your worth without waiting for someone else to validate it. It's holding space for your pain while also choosing to heal. Self-love isn't about thinking you're better than others — it's about not thinking you are less than anyone. It's not about ignoring your flaws but embracing your wholeness.

In practical terms, self-love means:

Setting boundaries without guilt.

Saying no to things that drain your energy.

Choosing rest without labeling it as laziness.

Celebrating your progress — even if it's not perfect.

13.2 Practical Ways to Practice Self-Love Daily

Self-love is built in everyday actions, not grand gestures. Here are some simple, practical ways to nurture self-love:

Morning Check-ins: Start your day by asking yourself how you feel. Check in with your emotional and physical state.

Positive Affirmations: Use phrases like "I am worthy," "I am doing my best," or "I deserve love." Speak these aloud while brushing your teeth or walking.

Nourishing Routines: Eat well, sleep adequately, hydrate — not as a punishment, but because you care.

Protecting Your Peace: Say no to toxic relationships and overcommitments. Value your energy.

Journaling: Write freely about your emotions, hopes, fears, and gratitude. It clears mental clutter and connects you with your inner world.

Celebrate Small Wins: Didn't snooze the alarm? Finished your to-do list? Celebrate it.

You don't have to wait to be perfect to love yourself. Start today. Love yourself in the becoming, not just in the achieving.

13.3 Mirror Exercise for Self-Validation

Sometimes the person we need the most validation from is ourselves. Not society. Not a loved one. Not a social media follower. Just you. That's where the mirror exercise becomes powerful — it gently brings you face-to-face with the most important relationship in your life: the one you have with yourself.

? What is the Mirror Exercise?

It's a simple yet transformative daily practice where you look at yourself in the mirror — not to judge your appearance, but to see yourself, speak to yourself, and build emotional intimacy within.

? How to Do the Mirror Exercise

Choose a quiet space where you won't be disturbed — ideally in the morning or right before bed.

Stand or sit in front of the mirror.

Look into your own eyes. Hold the gaze — not with criticism, but with compassion.

Take a deep breath.

Feel your presence. Let go of tension. This moment is only for you.

Speak kindly to yourself.

Say things like:

"I am proud of you."

"You are trying, and that is beautiful."

"You've been through so much, and yet here you are."

"You are enough. You've always been enough."

Name one thing you forgive yourself for.

Release self-blame. Say it out loud:

"I forgive myself for not knowing better then."

"I forgive myself for being hard on myself."

Name one thing you are proud of.

Acknowledge your growth, no matter how small:

"I'm proud of how I showed up for myself today."

"I'm proud that I didn't give up."

? Why This Exercise Matters

Most of us are quick to criticize ourselves in front of the mirror — judging our looks, weight, flaws. This exercise flips that pattern. Over time, it:

Builds self-trust

Heals low self-worth

Softens your inner critic

Connects you with your deeper self

Helps you develop emotional safety within

? Pro Tip:

If it feels awkward at first, that's okay. Most people aren't used to speaking gently to themselves. Keep going. Even 2 minutes a day can begin to shift how you see yourself.

A Final Whisper:

The world may not always affirm you. But you can choose to affirm yourself. You can choose to love, support, and stand by you. Every single day.

You are already worthy of your own love.

XI

Breaking Free from Fear

Understanding the Nature of Fear

Fear.

It's one of the most powerful emotions we experience. It protects us, warns us, even saves us — but too often, it also controls us.

Fear whispers:

"What if you fail?"

"What will they think?"

"You're not ready."

"You're not enough."

And when we believe these whispers, we start shrinking. We say no to opportunities, we silence our voices, we walk away from dreams — not because we're not capable, but because fear convinced us we aren't.

But let's pause here.

Let's strip fear of its power — not by pretending it doesn't exist, but by understanding what it really is.

? What Is Fear, Really?

Fear is an emotional response to a perceived threat. It's your brain's natural way of keeping you safe. Thousands of years ago, fear kept us alive by alerting us to danger — like wild animals or unsafe environments. But today, fear often shows up around emotional and social threats:

Rejection

Failure

Judgment

Change

The unknown

Here's the truth:

Fear is not the enemy.

Let me say that again — fear is not the enemy.

Fear only becomes a problem when it runs your life, when it decides for you.

? Two Kinds of Fear:

Protective Fear

This is healthy. It's the voice that says, "Don't touch fire." It guards your physical safety.

Limiting Fear

This is what holds you back from growth. It's the voice that says, "Don't speak up. Don't try. Don't shine."

Most of the fear we struggle with today is limiting fear. And we can challenge it. Gently. Consciously. Intentionally.

? A Real Talk Moment:

Think of all the things you haven't done because of fear.

The people you didn't approach.

The ideas you didn't share.

The goals you didn't pursue.

Not because you couldn't — but because fear convinced you not to try.

You deserve better than a life ruled by fear.

You deserve to trust your inner voice — even when your hands shake. Even when your knees tremble.

You don't need to be fearless to move forward.

You just need to be brave enough to take one step.

15.2 How Fear Manifests in Our Lives

Fear doesn't always come screaming.

Sometimes, it shows up quietly — dressed as hesitation, overthinking, perfectionism, or even procrastination.

We often imagine fear as something dramatic — like stage fright or panic. But the truth is, fear sneaks into everyday decisions. It hides behind excuses. It pretends to be logic. It wears masks.

Let's uncover some of the common ways fear shows up in our lives, so we can finally see it for what it is.

? Subtle Faces of Fear

Procrastination

"I'll do it tomorrow."

Sound familiar?

Sometimes, we're not lazy — we're scared. Scared to fail. Scared to be judged. Scared to realize we're not as ready as we thought.

Perfectionism

The idea that everything must be flawless before we can begin.

Fear whispers, "If it's not perfect, they'll laugh. You'll lose. Don't even try."

Overthinking

You analyze so much that you end up doing nothing. Every path feels risky, every step feels unsure.

People-Pleasing

Saying yes when you want to say no.

Smiling when you're breaking inside.

Why? Because fear tells you that if you're not agreeable, you'll be abandoned.

Staying "Comfortable"

Not taking risks. Not applying for the job. Not leaving the toxic relationship.

Because fear tells you it's safer to stay small than to fail trying.

? Heart-to-Heart Reflection:

We don't realize it, but fear can build an invisible cage around our lives.

And the scariest part?

We decorate that cage.

We make it look normal.

We convince ourselves we're just being cautious. But deep down, we know — we're playing small. And it hurts.

The moment we name our fear is the moment it starts losing control over us.

✍? Journal Prompt:

Grab your journal. Be raw. Be honest. Ask yourself:

What is one thing I've been avoiding because of fear?

How has fear stopped me from being fully me?

Write it out. Don't judge it. Just let it flow.

15.3 Rewriting Your Fear Narrative

Fear has a powerful voice in our minds. It often tells us stories — stories of doubt, limitation, and "what if" scenarios that hold us back from living fully. But here's the truth nobody tells you: You have the power to rewrite those stories. To change the narrative that fear has been feeding you for years.

Imagine fear as a broken record playing the same scary song over and over. Rewriting your fear narrative means changing that song — choosing words and thoughts that uplift you instead of tear you down.

? Why Rewriting Matters

When fear controls your story, you're stuck in a loop of "I can't," "I'm not enough," or "This is too risky." These beliefs create invisible walls, and you might not even realize they're there because fear convinces you they're "real" or "true."

Rewriting your narrative isn't about ignoring fear or pretending it doesn't exist. It's about acknowledging fear and gently telling it you're the one in charge now. It's about reclaiming your power, one thought at a time.

? How to Rewrite Your Fear Narrative

Catch the Fear Voice:

When you notice a fearful thought, pause. Write it down. For example, "I'm going to fail," or "I'm not good enough."

Challenge It:

Ask yourself: Is this really true? What evidence do I have? Often, fear exaggerates or lies. Maybe you failed once, but did you learn? Did you grow?

Create a New Story:

Replace the fearful thought with a positive, empowering one. Instead of "I will fail," say, "I will try my best, and that is enough." Instead of "I'm not good enough," say, "I am learning and growing every day."

Repeat and Reinforce:

Your brain will resist new stories at first. That's normal. Keep repeating your new narrative until it starts to feel natural.

Visualize Your Success:

Spend a few minutes each day imagining yourself succeeding despite fear. Feel the pride, the joy, and the confidence.

? A Heart-to-Heart with You

Changing your fear narrative takes courage. It's like facing a storm inside you and deciding to dance in the rain instead of running away. It's messy, it's uncomfortable, but it's also incredibly freeing.

You might stumble. You might have days when fear wins. That's okay. Progress isn't about perfection; it's about persistence. Each time you rewrite your fear story, you reclaim a piece of your power and step closer to the life you deserve.

✍? Reflection Exercise: Rewrite Your Fear Story

Take a moment now and write down one fear that's holding you back. Next to it, write a new empowering statement that challenges and replaces that fear.

Example:

Fear: "I'm not smart enough to succeed."

New Story: "I am capable of learning and growing every day."

Keep this somewhere visible. Read it daily. Let it remind you that you are the author of your story — not your fear.

Remember: Your fear is not your enemy — it's a signal that you're stepping out of your comfort zone and growing. Treat it with kindness, but don't let it control your journey.

15.4 Practical Exercises to Build Courage

Building courage is like strengthening a muscle — it takes practice, patience, and consistency. Courage doesn't mean the absence of fear; it means acting despite fear. Here are some practical exercises that can help you develop this powerful quality, step by step.

1. Take Small Risks Daily

Start with small actions that push you slightly out of your comfort zone. It could be speaking up in a meeting, trying a new hobby, or saying no to something you don't want to do. These small wins add up and build your confidence over time.

2. Practice Mindfulness and Grounding

Fear often spirals when your mind races with worst-case scenarios. Mindfulness practices — like deep breathing, meditation, or simply paying attention to your senses — can calm your nervous system and help you stay present. When you feel fear creeping in, ground yourself by noticing five things you see, four things you hear, three things you touch, two things you smell, and one thing you taste.

3. Visualize Success

Spend a few minutes daily imagining yourself facing your fear and coming out strong on the other side. Visualization helps train your brain to expect positive outcomes and prepares you emotionally to handle challenges.

4. Create a Courage Journal

Write down moments when you acted courageously — big or small. Reflect on how it felt, what you learned, and how you can build on that experience. When fear feels overwhelming, revisit your courage journal to remind yourself of your inner strength.

5. Use Affirmations to Empower Yourself

Repeat affirmations that encourage bravery, such as:

"I am brave, even when I feel scared."

"Every step forward is a victory."

"I have faced challenges before and I can do it again."

Say these aloud in front of the mirror or write them down in your journal.

6. Seek Support and Share Your Journey

Courage grows when you don't walk alone. Talk to trusted friends, mentors, or counselors about your fears and your efforts to overcome them. Their encouragement can provide motivation and perspective.

A Heartfelt Reminder

Building courage isn't a race — it's a lifelong journey. Some days will feel easier than others, and that's perfectly normal. Celebrate every brave step you take, no matter how small. Each act of courage strengthens your spirit and opens new doors to growth and freedom.

Reflection Task:

Pick one courage-building exercise from this list to try today. Reflect on how it made you feel and write about your experience. Notice any changes in your mindset or behavior, even if they are subtle.

XII

Building Support Systems

Why Support Systems Matter

Life's challenges become more manageable when we have a strong support system around us. Whether it's family, friends, mentors, or community groups, support systems provide emotional strength, practical help, and encouragement when we need it most.

Sometimes, we try to face everything alone, thinking it's a sign of strength. But real strength lies in recognizing when you need others and allowing them to be there for you. Having people who believe in you, listen to you without judgment, and stand by you through thick and thin makes the journey less lonely and more hopeful.

Support systems can:

Offer different perspectives to help solve problems.

Celebrate your victories, big or small.

Help you stay accountable to your goals.

Provide a safe space to express your feelings and fears.

Boost your confidence by reminding you of your worth.

Building your support system means intentionally surrounding yourself with people who lift you up and inspire you to grow. It also means learning to ask for help without guilt and being open to receiving care.

Reflection Task:

List three people or groups in your life who support you. How do they help you? Write down ways you can strengthen these relationships or reach out to new support networks.

16.2 How to Find and Build Your Support Network

Building a support system doesn't happen overnight—it takes time, effort, and sometimes courage. But the rewards are worth it. When you have people who genuinely care about your growth and well-being, life feels less overwhelming.

Start with Who You Have

Look around and identify people who have been there for you in the past. They could be family members, friends, teachers, colleagues, or even neighbors. Sometimes, we overlook the support that's already present because we get caught up in our struggles.

Reach Out and Communicate

Building a support network starts with reaching out. It could be as simple as sending a message saying, "I could really use someone to talk to," or inviting someone for a coffee. Vulnerability is scary, but it's also a bridge that connects hearts.

Join Communities and Groups

Look for groups, clubs, or organizations aligned with your interests or goals. This could be a book club, a fitness class, a career workshop, or online forums. Being around like-minded people provides not just support but inspiration.

Seek Mentors and Role Models

Mentors can offer guidance based on experience and wisdom. Don't hesitate to approach someone you admire and ask for advice. Remember, mentors aren't always formal; sometimes, they're people who inspire you simply by how they live.

Give Back and Be Supportive Too

Support systems thrive on mutual care. When you support others, you build stronger bonds and create a positive cycle. Listen actively, celebrate others' successes, and offer help where you can.

Set Healthy Boundaries

Not everyone in your life will be part of your support system, and that's okay. Recognize relationships that drain your energy or bring negativity, and set boundaries to protect your peace.

Reflection Task:

Write down three new ways you can expand or deepen your support system. Who can you reach out to? What groups can you join? How can you offer support to others?

16.3 Maintaining Healthy Relationships

Once you have built your support network, maintaining those relationships becomes just as important. Healthy relationships are like a garden—they need regular care, attention, and nurturing to flourish.

Communication Is Key

Honest and open communication is the foundation of any healthy relationship. Share your feelings and thoughts sincerely, and encourage others to do the same. Listen not just to respond, but to truly understand.

Practice Empathy and Patience

Everyone has their own struggles and imperfections. Try to see things from their perspective and be patient during tough times. Compassion strengthens bonds and creates a safe space for both parties.

Respect Boundaries

Just as you need your personal space, respect the boundaries of others. Healthy relationships thrive when both sides honor each other's limits without judgment or resentment.

Celebrate Together

Take time to celebrate each other's achievements, big or small. Sharing joy builds positive energy and reinforces the support system.

Resolve Conflicts Gracefully

Disagreements are natural but should be handled with respect. Avoid blame or harsh words. Instead, focus on finding solutions and understanding each other's needs.

Invest Time and Effort

Relationships require ongoing effort. Regular check-ins, shared activities, or simple gestures like sending a thoughtful message go a long way in keeping connections strong.

Know When to Let Go

Sometimes, relationships become toxic or draining. Recognize when a connection is harming your well-being and have the courage to distance yourself if needed.

Reflection Task:

Think about your current relationships. What are three ways you can improve communication or nurture these bonds? Are there any relationships that need boundaries or reconsideration?

16.4 Reflection Exercise: Mapping Your Support System

Understanding and visualizing your support system is a powerful step toward strengthening your emotional well-being. This exercise will help you identify who is in your circle, how they support you, and where you might want to build new connections.

How to Do the Support System Mapping Exercise:

Draw a Circle:

Take a blank sheet of paper and draw a large circle in the middle. This represents you.

Add Circles Around You:

Around your circle, draw smaller circles to represent people in your life. Start with those closest to you — family, best friends, mentors — and then add acquaintances or community members further out.

Label Each Circle:

Write the names or roles of these people inside each circle. Be honest about how close you feel to them.

Identify Types of Support:

Next to each circle, write down the kind of support they provide. It could be emotional (someone who listens), practical (someone who helps you with tasks), motivational (someone who encourages your goals), or spiritual (someone who shares your beliefs).

Reflect on Balance:

Look at your map. Do you have a balanced mix of support? Are there areas where you feel isolated or lacking connection? Which relationships feel strong, and which might need work?

Set Goals:

Based on your reflection, set one or two goals to strengthen your support system. Maybe it's reaching out to an old friend, joining a community group, or setting boundaries in a draining relationship.

Why This Exercise Matters

Visualizing your support system helps you appreciate the people who stand by you and recognize gaps you might want to fill. Building a strong network is not about quantity but quality — those who genuinely care and uplift you.

Remember, you don't have to walk your journey alone. Support is out there — sometimes you just need to take the first step.

Talk With the Reader:

This map isn't static. As you grow and change, so will your support system. Be patient with yourself and others. Reach out when you need to, and don't hesitate to let go of what no longer serves your peace

XIII
Building Resilience

What Resilience Really Means

Resilience is often seen as a superhuman ability to bounce back from adversity without breaking. But in reality, resilience is much more human and accessible than that. It's not about being invincible; it's about being flexible — bending but not breaking. It's about acknowledging pain, accepting hardship, and still choosing to move forward.

Think of resilience as a muscle. It grows stronger every time you face a challenge and choose to keep going. It's built through experience, mindset, and support — not something you are just born with.

Resilience doesn't mean you won't feel overwhelmed or discouraged. It means you don't let those feelings define you or keep you stuck. It's your ability to face difficulties with courage, learn from them, and adapt.

Key qualities of resilience include:

Emotional awareness: Knowing your feelings without being overwhelmed.

Optimism: Believing that things can improve.

Self-efficacy: Trusting your ability to handle challenges.

Flexibility: Being open to change and new ways of coping.

Support-seeking: Reaching out to others when needed.

17.2 Developing a Resilient Mindset

Building resilience starts with the way you think about yourself and your challenges. The mindset you choose can either hold you back or empower you to keep going, even when things feel tough.

A resilient mindset is about:

Seeing setbacks as temporary, not permanent. Instead of thinking, "I failed and I'm a failure," try, "This didn't work out, but I can learn and try again."

Believing in your ability to grow. You might not have all the answers now, but you have the strength and resources to figure things out.

Accepting that pain and discomfort are part of growth. Life isn't always easy, and resilience means riding through the tough moments without losing hope.

Focusing on what you can control. You might not control every situation, but you can control your response, your attitude, and your effort.

This mindset is not something you develop overnight. It takes practice. When you notice negative thoughts creeping in, challenge them gently. Ask yourself:

Is this thought true?

Is it helpful?

What would I say to a friend feeling this way?

Over time, you'll notice a shift in how you face difficulties. You'll start to view challenges as opportunities to learn, rather than threats to avoid.

Remember, developing a resilient mindset is a journey, not a destination. Be patient with yourself and celebrate small wins along the way.

17.3 Practical Ways to Build Resilience

Resilience isn't just a feeling—it's a skill you can strengthen with daily habits and conscious actions. Here are some practical steps you can start today:

Build Strong Connections

Surround yourself with people who support you, listen without judgment, and encourage your growth. Sharing your struggles with trusted friends or mentors can lighten your load and provide new perspectives.

Practice Self-Compassion

Be kind to yourself when things don't go as planned. Talk to yourself like you would to a friend. Replace self-criticism with understanding and encouragement.

Set Realistic Goals

Break your big challenges into smaller, achievable steps. Celebrate progress, no matter how small—it fuels motivation and builds confidence.

Develop Problem-Solving Skills

When faced with a challenge, pause and think through possible solutions. Taking action, even small steps, helps you feel more in control.

Maintain a Positive Outlook

Try to focus on what's going right or what you can learn from every experience. Gratitude journaling, even for simple things, can shift your mindset over time.

Take Care of Your Body

Physical health and mental resilience are connected. Regular exercise, enough sleep, and nutritious food help your mind stay sharp and calm under pressure.

Embrace Flexibility

Life is unpredictable. Being willing to adapt your plans and try new approaches makes it easier to bounce back from setbacks.

These strategies aren't magic fixes but steady practices that help you build mental and emotional strength over time. Start small, stay consistent, and watch your resilience grow.

17.4 Resilience-Building Exercises

Building resilience requires practice and reflection. Here are some exercises to help you strengthen your inner strength:

Exercise 1: Reflect on Past Challenges

Take a moment to write about a difficult situation you faced in the past. How did you overcome it? What did you learn about yourself? Recognizing your past resilience can boost your confidence for current struggles.

Exercise 2: Create a Resilience Toolbox

List activities, people, or thoughts that help you feel calm and strong. This could include listening to music, talking to a trusted friend, taking deep breaths, or reading inspirational quotes. Keep this list handy to turn to when you feel overwhelmed.

Exercise 3: Practice Mindfulness

Spend 5–10 minutes each day focusing on your breath or a calming image. Mindfulness helps you stay grounded in the present, reducing anxiety about the future or regrets about the past.

Exercise 4: Affirmation Statements

Write and repeat positive affirmations like "I am capable," "I can handle challenges," or "Every setback is a step forward." Say them aloud in front of a mirror daily to reinforce your belief in yourself.

Try to incorporate these exercises regularly to build your resilience muscle. Remember, resilience grows with patience and persistence.

18.1 Understanding Healthy Relationships

Healthy relationships are the foundation of a happy and balanced life. Whether it's with family, friends, or romantic partners, the quality of your relationships directly impacts your emotional and mental well-being.

A healthy relationship is based on:

Mutual respect: Both people value each other's feelings and boundaries.

Trust: Feeling safe to be yourself without fear of judgment or betrayal.

Open communication: Sharing thoughts and feelings honestly and listening actively.

Support: Encouraging each other's growth and being there in difficult times.

Equality: Both partners share responsibility and decision-making fairly.

In contrast, unhealthy relationships might involve control, disrespect, dishonesty, or emotional neglect, which can drain your energy and self-worth.

Recognizing what makes a relationship healthy helps you build stronger connections and avoid toxic patterns.

18.2 Signs of Unhealthy Relationships

Relationships are meant to nourish us, to help us grow, and to provide comfort and support. But sometimes, the people closest to us may unintentionally—or even intentionally—cause pain and confusion. Recognizing the signs of an unhealthy relationship is one of the bravest steps you can take toward reclaiming your peace and self-worth.

So, what does an unhealthy relationship look like?

It doesn't always scream in obvious ways. Sometimes, it quietly erodes your confidence, your happiness, and your sense of self. Here are the key signs to watch for, in yourself and others:

1. Lack of Respect

Respect is the foundation of every healthy relationship. If your thoughts, feelings, or boundaries are ignored or mocked, it's a red flag. You should never feel small or invalidated by someone who claims to care for you. When respect is missing, it feels like walking on eggshells—never knowing when the next hurtful comment will come.

2. Constant Criticism or Judgment

We all need honest feedback, but when criticism is constant and harsh, it chips away at your self-esteem. Instead of encouragement, you feel like you're always failing or not enough. This type of relationship feeds your insecurities and leaves you doubting your worth.

3. Control and Manipulation

Healthy relationships thrive on freedom and trust, not control. If someone tries to dictate where you go, who you see, or what you do, it's a sign of control. Manipulation might come disguised as guilt-tripping, gaslighting (making you question your reality), or emotional blackmail. This is not love—it's a trap that slowly steals your independence.

4. Dishonesty and Secrets

Trust is sacred. When lies or hidden truths become common, trust breaks. You might feel confused, suspicious, or anxious because you can't predict what's real or fake. A relationship without honesty is built on shaky ground and leaves you constantly on edge.

5. Emotional Exhaustion

If you consistently feel drained, anxious, or sad after interactions, your relationship may be toxic. Relationships should energize and inspire you, not leave you depleted. Pay attention to how you feel—not just during happy moments, but after the hard conversations and disagreements too.

6. Unequal Effort and Sacrifice

Love and friendship require effort from both sides. If you find yourself always giving—whether it's time, energy, or emotional support—but rarely receiving the same in return, the balance is off. Feeling unappreciated or taken for granted can be deeply hurtful.

7. Isolation from Others

One of the sneakiest signs of an unhealthy relationship is when you start to lose contact with friends or family. If someone pressures you to avoid others, controls who you talk to, or makes you feel guilty for spending time away, it's a tactic to isolate and weaken you.

8. Fear and Silence

Fear is never a part of healthy love. If you feel scared to speak up, share your feelings, or be your authentic self, the relationship is damaging you. Silence born out of fear creates walls where openness and understanding should be.

Why is it important to recognize these signs?

Because awareness is the first step toward change. You deserve relationships that lift you up, not tear you down. You deserve to be treated with kindness, honesty, and respect.

If you're reading this and nodding along, feeling a heavy ache in your chest—know that your feelings are valid. It's okay to acknowledge that something isn't right. It's okay to want better. And it's okay to take steps to protect your heart, even if that means stepping away.

Remember: Protecting yourself is an act of courage, not selfishness. Choosing your peace over pain is one of the most powerful gifts you can give yourself.

18.3 How to Set Boundaries

Setting boundaries can feel scary—especially if you've spent a long time ignoring your own needs or if you fear upsetting others. But boundaries are not walls to shut people out; they are bridges that protect your well-being and help build honest, respectful connections.

Think of boundaries as your personal limits. They tell others what is okay and what is not okay in how they treat you, and they give you space to breathe, heal, and grow.

So, how do you start setting boundaries? Here's a simple guide:

1. Tune In to Your Feelings

Your body and mind give you signals when something feels wrong—like tension in your chest, anxiety, anger, or sadness. These feelings are your inner compass pointing out where boundaries may need to be drawn. Pay close attention to when you feel uncomfortable, overwhelmed, or disrespected.

2. Know Your Limits

Before you can communicate boundaries, you need to understand what your limits are. What behaviors or situations drain your energy? What makes you feel unsafe or disrespected? What are your deal breakers? Being clear with yourself is the foundation of clear communication with others.

3. Start Small and Specific

You don't have to overhaul your relationships overnight. Begin with small, manageable boundaries. For example, if a friend often calls late at night and it disturbs your rest, say, "I need to keep my phone off after 10 PM for better sleep." Being specific helps avoid confusion.

4. Use "I" Statements

When you express your boundaries, speak from your experience to avoid sounding accusatory. For example:

"I feel overwhelmed when plans change last minute."

"I need some time to myself after work to recharge."

This approach invites understanding instead of defensiveness.

5. Be Consistent and Firm

Boundaries are only effective when respected. If you set a limit, stand by it. If someone crosses it, gently remind them of your boundary. It's okay to say no—your needs matter. Consistency teaches others how to treat you.

6. Expect Mixed Reactions

Not everyone will respond positively at first. Some may feel hurt or confused because your boundaries disrupt old patterns. That's okay. Remember, you're not responsible for their feelings—only for your own well-being.

7. Practice Self-Compassion

Setting boundaries can stir guilt or fear, especially if you're used to putting others first. Remind yourself that caring for yourself is necessary and healthy. You deserve to be treated with respect and kindness.

8. Seek Support

If setting boundaries feels overwhelming, talk to someone you trust—a friend, counselor, or mentor. Sometimes, just knowing you have support gives you the strength to say what you need.

A quick reminder: Boundaries are a form of self-respect. They teach others how to love and respect you. Without boundaries, you risk losing yourself trying to please others.

Reflection Question:

What is one boundary you can start setting today, no matter how small? How will it help protect your peace?

18.4 Healthy Relationship Habits

Relationships are like gardens — they need regular care, attention, and nurturing to thrive. Whether it's with family, friends, partners, or even colleagues, healthy relationships enrich our lives and give us strength. But like any garden, they also need boundaries, honesty, and respect to flourish.

Here are some habits that can help you build and maintain healthy, loving relationships:

1. Open and Honest Communication

Being honest doesn't mean being harsh or blunt. It means sharing your thoughts and feelings clearly and kindly. When you communicate openly, you build trust. Don't bottle up what's bothering you—find gentle ways to express it.

2. Active Listening

Listening is more than just hearing words. It means truly paying attention, without interrupting or planning your response while the other person is talking. Show that you value what they say by nodding, making eye contact, and asking thoughtful questions.

3. Respecting Differences

Everyone is unique, and disagreements are natural. Respect others' opinions, even if they differ from yours. Healthy relationships don't require agreement on everything — they require acceptance and understanding.

4. Supporting Each Other's Growth

Encourage your loved ones to pursue their dreams and goals. Celebrate their successes and be a source of comfort in tough times. When both people grow individually, the relationship becomes stronger.

5. Quality Time Together

In our busy lives, spending meaningful time together is precious. Whether it's a walk, a chat over tea, or a shared hobby, make time to connect regularly. These moments build emotional closeness.

6. Expressing Appreciation

Never underestimate the power of saying "thank you," "I appreciate you," or "You mean a lot to me." Small words of gratitude and kindness nurture feelings of love and belonging.

7. Healthy Conflict Resolution

Conflicts are inevitable, but how you handle them matters. Approach disagreements calmly, avoid blame, and focus on finding solutions rather than winning arguments. Take breaks if emotions run too high and revisit the conversation later.

8. Setting and Respecting Boundaries

Remember what we talked about earlier? Boundaries are essential in healthy relationships. Respect others' limits and clearly communicate your own. This mutual respect keeps relationships balanced and fulfilling.

9. Forgiveness and Letting Go

Holding grudges only weighs you down. Forgiveness doesn't mean forgetting or excusing hurtful behavior; it means releasing yourself from the burden of resentment. Forgive to free your heart and move forward.

Remember: Healthy relationships require effort from both sides, but you deserve relationships where your heart feels safe, seen, and cherished. Don't settle for less.

Reflection Question:

Think about one relationship in your life — what's one habit you can cultivate to make it healthier and more joyful?

XIV

Cultivating Gratitude Understanding Gratitude and Its Impact

Understanding Gratitude and Its Impact

Gratitude is more than just saying "thank you" when someone hands you something or does a favor. It's a deep feeling of appreciation — a warm recognition of the good things in our lives, big or small. Sometimes, when life feels overwhelming or unfair, gratitude can feel distant or even impossible. But that's exactly when it matters the most.

When you practice gratitude, you are rewiring your brain to focus on what's working rather than what's missing. It helps shift your mindset from scarcity to abundance, from frustration to acceptance. And this shift has a ripple effect — it can improve your mood, relationships, and even your physical health.

Gratitude doesn't mean ignoring your struggles or pretending everything is perfect. It means acknowledging your reality while still finding light in the shadows. It's a quiet, powerful act of resilience.

In many cultures and spiritual traditions, gratitude is seen as a key to happiness and inner peace. Science backs this up too — studies show that people who regularly practice gratitude experience less stress, better sleep, and stronger immune systems.

Gratitude opens the door to joy, even on tough days.

19.2 Simple Daily Gratitude Practices

Starting a gratitude practice doesn't have to be complicated or time-consuming. In fact, the simplest habits can create the biggest shifts. What matters is consistency and genuine feeling — it's not about perfection or fancy rituals.

Here are some practical, easy ways to weave gratitude into your daily life:

1. Gratitude Journaling:

Each day, write down three things you are grateful for. They can be as simple as the morning chai you enjoyed, a smile from a stranger, or the fact that you woke up healthy. Over time, you'll start to notice patterns — things you might have overlooked before — and your heart will expand.

2. Gratitude Reminders:

Set reminders on your phone or place sticky notes around your home with prompts like "What am I grateful for right now?" These small nudges can help bring your attention back to gratitude throughout the day.

3. Thank You Notes:

Write a quick note, text, or message to someone who made a difference in your day — a friend, a family member, a colleague, or even yourself. Expressing thanks deepens connections and spreads positivity.

4. Mindful Moments:

Pause for a minute or two during your day — maybe while waiting in line or before meals — and silently acknowledge one thing you appreciate at that moment. It can be your breath, the weather, or the food on your plate.

5. Gratitude Walks:

Take a walk outside and mentally list the things around you that you feel grateful for — the trees, the sky, the sounds, or even your own strength to move. Nature has a way of grounding us and opening our hearts.

The key is to make gratitude a habit — a natural part of your day — rather than a forced chore. When you start to focus on what's good, you'll notice your worries and doubts lose some of their power.

Remember, gratitude is a muscle — the more you practice, the stronger it gets.

19.3 How Gratitude Changes Your Brain and Life

Gratitude isn't just a feel-good emotion — it actually rewires your brain and transforms your life in powerful ways. Science has proven what many wise people have known for centuries: practicing gratitude regularly creates real, positive changes inside you.

Here's how gratitude impacts your brain and overall well-being:

1. Activates the Reward System:

When you express gratitude, your brain's reward centers light up, releasing dopamine and serotonin — the "happy chemicals." This natural boost helps improve your mood and makes you feel more content, reducing anxiety and depression.

2. Strengthens Neural Pathways:

Like any habit, gratitude creates stronger neural connections in your brain. The more you practice it, the easier it becomes to notice and focus on the positive in life — even when things get tough.

3. Lowers Stress Hormones:

Regular gratitude practice lowers levels of cortisol, the hormone linked to stress. This means your body feels calmer, your heart health improves, and your immune system gets a boost.

4. Enhances Resilience:

By focusing on what's good, you build mental strength to face challenges. Gratitude shifts your mindset from victimhood to empowerment, helping you recover faster from setbacks.

5. Improves Relationships:

Gratitude helps you appreciate others more deeply, leading to stronger bonds, more empathy, and increased feelings of connection and support.

6. Increases Mindfulness:

Gratitude encourages you to live in the present moment. When you focus on what you have now, you're less likely to dwell on regrets or worries about the future.

Why does this matter? Because every thought you have shapes your reality. By rewiring your brain to focus on gratitude, you gradually change the way you experience life — from confusion and struggle to clarity and peace.

So, even when life feels chaotic or unfair, your daily gratitude practice becomes a lifeline — a reminder that there is still light, still hope, and still reason to keep moving forward.

19.4 Reflection Exercise: Your Gratitude Journal

Starting a gratitude journal is one of the simplest and most powerful ways to bring more positivity into your life. This exercise invites you to slow down, reflect, and write down the things you are thankful for — big or small.

Why keep a gratitude journal?

Writing gratitude daily helps you focus your mind on the positive. It trains your brain to notice the good around you, even when life feels hard.

This simple act can reduce stress, improve sleep, boost mood, and increase overall happiness.

How to Start Your Gratitude Journal:

Choose Your Medium:

Pick a notebook, journal app, or even a simple piece of paper—whatever feels easiest and most comfortable for you.

Set a Time:

Commit to writing in your journal every day. It can be in the morning to set a positive tone for the day, or before bed to reflect on the day's blessings.

Write Three Things You're Grateful For:

These don't have to be big events. They can be as simple as a warm cup of tea, a smile from a stranger, or a moment of peace.

Be Specific:

Instead of writing "I'm grateful for my family," try "I'm grateful for the way my sister listened to me today." Specificity makes gratitude more meaningful.

Reflect on How These Things Make You Feel:

Write a sentence or two about how these blessings impact your mood or your day.

Sample Gratitude Journal Entry:

Today, I am grateful for the gentle rain that cooled the afternoon — it made me feel calm and refreshed. I'm grateful for my friend's encouraging message, which reminded me I'm not alone. I appreciate the quiet moment I had to sit and breathe deeply.

Tips for Keeping Your Gratitude Journal Alive:

Don't worry about perfection: This is for you, not anyone else. Write freely.

Mix it up: Add drawings, poems, or quotes that inspire you.

Review periodically: Reread past entries when you feel down — it can lift your spirits instantly.

Be patient: Like any habit, gratitude journaling gets easier and more powerful with time.

Remember, this journal is a safe space — a personal sanctuary to nurture your heart and mind. Start today, even if you write just one line. Over time, you'll build a treasure trove of positivity to carry you through life's ups and downs.

Chapter 20: Forgiveness — Releasing the Past

20.2 Why We Struggle to Forgive

Forgiveness sounds beautiful — but the truth is, it's one of the hardest things we're ever asked to do. And if you're struggling to forgive, you're not weak... you're human.

There are many reasons why forgiveness feels like an impossible mountain to climb. Let's talk about some of them — not with judgment, but with understanding.

1. The Pain Feels Too Deep

Some wounds are not just scratches on the surface — they cut into our identity, our sense of safety, our self-worth. When the hurt runs deep, the idea of letting it go can feel like betrayal. You may wonder, "If I forgive them, does it mean what they did was okay?" The answer is no. Forgiving doesn't minimize your pain; it validates it... and then frees you from it.

2. We're Still Waiting for an Apology

Sometimes the person who hurt us doesn't say sorry. Or worse, they act like nothing happened. That makes forgiveness feel unjust. "Why should I forgive them when they haven't even acknowledged what they did?" The hard truth? Some people will never apologize. But your healing doesn't have to depend on their words. Forgiveness is about your peace — not their guilt.

3. We Tie Forgiveness to Reconnection

Many believe forgiving means reconnecting — letting the person back into your life. But that's not true. You can forgive and still walk away. Forgiveness is an internal act; reconciliation is an external one. You can wish someone healing and still choose never to let them hurt you again.

4. We Feel Like We're Losing Control

Holding onto anger can feel powerful — like a shield. Releasing it might feel like giving up control. But in reality, it's anger that controls you. When you forgive, you take back your power. You decide how you move forward, not your pain.

5. We Don't Know How to Forgive Ourselves

Sometimes the hardest person to forgive is the one in the mirror. Maybe you blame yourself for staying too long, speaking too little, ignoring red flags, or believing lies. But please hear this: You did what you could with what you knew at the time. Self-forgiveness is where real healing begins.

It's okay if forgiveness doesn't come easily. That's part of the journey. Be patient with yourself. Let your heart heal at its own pace.

20.3 The Myths About Forgiveness

Forgiveness is often misunderstood. We're fed so many ideas about what it "should" look like — and most of them only make the process harder.

Let's gently unpack some of these myths, because when we clear away the confusion, we make space for true healing.

Myth 1: Forgiveness Means Forgetting

You've probably heard the phrase "forgive and forget." But let's be honest — forgetting isn't always possible. And more importantly, it isn't necessary. Forgiveness isn't about erasing memories; it's about releasing the hold those memories have on you. You can remember and still move forward. You can acknowledge the hurt without letting it define you.

Myth 2: You Must Forgive Immediately

Healing doesn't work on a timer. There's no rush. Sometimes we force ourselves to forgive because we think it's what "strong" or "spiritual" people do. But forced forgiveness is not real forgiveness — it's emotional bypassing. Give yourself time. Forgiveness is a process, not a performance.

Myth 3: Forgiveness Equals Reconciliation

This one causes the most confusion. You do not have to reconcile with someone to forgive them. Forgiveness is internal — it happens in your heart. Reconciliation is external — it happens through mutual effort, trust, and repair. You can forgive and still choose boundaries, distance, or even complete disconnection. That doesn't make you cold — it makes you wise.

Myth 4: Forgiveness Makes You Weak

In reality, forgiveness is one of the most courageous acts you'll ever perform. It takes strength to say, "I'm no longer giving this pain the power to poison my peace." Letting go doesn't mean you're weak. It means you're choosing freedom over bitterness. That's power.

Myth 5: You Can Only Forgive Once You Feel Ready

Sometimes we wait for the right feeling — for the anger to dissolve or the pain to fade. But the truth is, forgiveness often comes before the feeling. It's a decision, a choice. And sometimes, that choice is the very thing that opens the door to healing emotions.

Let go of the myths. They only make the journey harder. Your forgiveness doesn't have to look like anyone else's. It just has to be real. And real begins with you.

20.4 A Path to Forgiveness: Small Steps Toward Healing

Forgiveness can feel like a mountain — distant, towering, and too heavy to climb. But the truth is, you don't need to leap to the top. You only need to take one small, honest step at a time.

There is no perfect script or timeline for forgiveness. Everyone's journey is different. But these gentle steps can guide your heart toward healing, without forcing you to rush or pretend.

Step 1: Acknowledge the Hurt Honestly

Start by naming what happened. What did you feel? Betrayal, abandonment, humiliation, fear? Don't sugarcoat it. Honesty is where healing begins. Sometimes writing it down, speaking it aloud to someone you trust, or just admitting it to yourself is a powerful first step.

Step 2: Allow Yourself to Feel Everything

Forgiveness doesn't mean bypassing emotions. Cry if you need to. Get angry. Feel sad. You're allowed to grieve the loss of trust, the innocence taken, the peace disturbed. Emotions are not obstacles — they are messengers. Let them speak.

Step 3: Understand the Weight You Carry

Unforgiveness is like dragging a heavy suitcase everywhere you go. It tires you, even if you pretend it's not there. Ask yourself gently: Is holding onto this pain serving me anymore? Sometimes, realizing how heavy the load is becomes the motivation to begin setting it down.

Step 4: Separate the Person from the Act

This is difficult but powerful. Try to see the person who hurt you as more than the moment they failed you. It doesn't excuse their behavior, but it can help you release the bitterness. Often, people hurt others from their own wounds, fears, and ignorance.

You're not just forgiving what they did — you're freeing yourself from why it's still hurting you.

Step 5: Make a Choice — Not a Feeling

Forgiveness doesn't always come with warm feelings. It's a choice you make, even when your heart still aches. Say to yourself, "I choose to let go of this burden so I can heal, not so they can feel better."

You may need to make that choice again and again — and that's okay. Forgiveness can be a repeated decision.

Step 6: Reclaim Your Power

When you forgive, you are not losing control — you are regaining it. You're no longer letting what someone did in the past control your present. You're choosing peace over pain. That's not weakness. That's strength. That's maturity. That's freedom.

Step 7: Begin to Release

You don't have to forget, reconcile, or erase the past. But maybe, day by day, you can loosen the grip. You can say, "This happened. It hurt. But I'm choosing not to let it define me anymore." That's how healing begins — not with dramatic gestures, but with quiet, brave decisions.

Forgiveness is a gift you give yourself first. It's not easy. But it is possible — and it's worth it. Not because the person who hurt you deserves peace... but because you do.

20.5 Reflection Exercise: Writing a Forgiveness Letter

Sometimes the pain lives quietly inside us — unspoken, unhealed. We carry it in our minds, our hearts, and even our bodies. One of the most powerful ways to begin releasing that pain is through writing.

Writing a forgiveness letter isn't about sending it. It's not about confrontation or closure from someone else. It's about you. About letting your truth pour out. About emptying what's heavy and giving yourself a safe space to feel, express, and begin to let go.

How to Write a Forgiveness Letter:

You don't have to be a writer. You just have to be honest.

Start with their name, or just "To the one who hurt me..."

This sets the tone. It helps you bring focus to the person or situation that needs healing.

Describe what happened.

Be clear. Say what they did or what didn't happen that caused you pain. Let your truth speak, without censoring.

"You lied to me when I needed honesty. You made me feel like my voice didn't matter. You weren't there when I needed support."

Share how it made you feel.

Let your emotions surface. Write the words you were never able to say out loud.

"I felt abandoned. I felt worthless. I lost trust, not just in you, but in myself. I carried shame, even though it wasn't mine to carry."

Write what you needed then.

Maybe you needed love, an apology, protection, truth, care. Write it. Give voice to the unmet need.

Decide if you are ready to forgive — and write that.

You can say:

"I'm not ready to forgive yet, but I want to get there."

"I am choosing to forgive you, not because you asked, but because I need peace."

"I forgive you, and I release this pain."

End with compassion — for yourself.

Even if you're angry, close the letter with a reminder to yourself that you deserve healing.

"I am stronger than this pain. I am worthy of peace. I choose to grow, even through this."

You can keep the letter, burn it, rip it up, or read it aloud. The healing comes in the writing, not the outcome.

This exercise may feel emotional. That's okay. It means your heart is opening. You're honoring your pain and beginning to release it with intention and grace.

Forgiveness isn't about forgetting or pretending. It's about freeing your spirit to move forward.

XV
Embracing Your Voice — Speaking Up with Confidence

Why Your Voice Matters

Your voice is more than just sound — it is your truth, your power, and your identity. It holds your beliefs, your dreams, your emotions. But for many of us, especially women and young individuals, the world has taught us to silence our voices — to stay "polite," "quiet," or "safe."

But you were not born to be invisible. Your thoughts, your ideas, and your experiences matter. Whether you're speaking up in a classroom, a workplace, at home, or on a public stage — your voice has the potential to change not just your life, but also the lives of others who hear it.

When you speak, you make space for your truth. And when you do that, you also give others permission to do the same. Confidence isn't about never feeling afraid — it's about choosing to speak anyway, despite the fear.

You don't have to be loud. You don't have to be perfect. You just have to be authentic.

Your voice deserves to be heard — not someday, but now.

21.2 Overcoming the Fear of Speaking Up

Fear is a quiet thief. It steals our words before we can say them. It convinces us that we're not smart enough, not strong enough, not worthy of being heard. And so we stay silent — not because we have nothing to say, but because we are afraid to say it.

But let's be honest: this fear isn't baseless. Maybe you were once laughed at when you spoke. Maybe someone interrupted you, dismissed your thoughts, or told you to "stay in your place." Maybe the world hasn't always been kind to your voice. That pain is real — and you deserve to acknowledge it.

But now, it's time to ask: Will you let that fear define you forever?

Here's the truth:

Your voice is your power. If it shakes, let it shake. If your hands tremble, let them tremble. That's not weakness — that's bravery in action.

Everyone starts somewhere. No one is born confident. Confidence is built — one small, courageous act at a time.

Mistakes don't make you unworthy. You might stumble. You might forget your words. That's okay. You're still worthy of speaking.

Try these steps to slowly overcome the fear:

Start small. Speak up in a safe space. Share your opinion with a friend or during a group activity.

Practice affirmations. Repeat: "My voice matters. My story is important. I deserve to be heard."

Breathe through the fear. When nerves rise, pause. Take a deep breath. Ground yourself. Then speak.

Prepare when possible. If you're speaking in public or in a meeting, write down your key points. Preparation builds confidence.

Visualize success. Close your eyes and imagine yourself speaking with calm strength. Feel it. Believe it.

Celebrate every effort. Whether you spoke a single sentence or delivered a speech — honor your courage.

Fear doesn't disappear overnight. But each time you choose to speak — even when it's uncomfortable — you grow stronger. One day, you'll look back and be amazed at how far you've come.

21.3 Finding and Honoring Your Unique Voice

Your voice is more than just sound — it's your truth, your energy, your essence. It carries your lived experiences, your dreams, your values. And the world doesn't need another copy of someone else. The world needs you — in your most honest, imperfect, radiant form.

Yet, so often, we hide our voices. We mimic others, water ourselves down, or silence our truths out of fear of judgment. We think, "What if they don't like what I have to say?" But the better question is — What if they never get to hear the real you because you never gave yourself the permission to speak as you are?

Your voice is not a mistake. It's your superpower.

You don't need to sound like a TED speaker or speak with polished grammar to be valuable. What you need is honesty. What you need is courage. What you need is you.

Here's how you begin to find and honor your voice:

1. Listen to Yourself First

Before you speak to the world, spend time listening to your inner world. What do you believe in? What angers you? What inspires you? Your voice stems from your truth — but you can't express it if you don't know it.

Try this: Write freely for 10 minutes every day. Let your thoughts pour out without editing. Over time, you'll start to recognize recurring themes — your inner compass.

2. Stop Comparing Your Voice to Others

Someone else might speak louder, use fancier words, or appear more confident. But that doesn't make their voice more worthy than yours. Their path is theirs. Yours is yours.

Comparison kills authenticity. Let it go. You weren't born to echo — you were born to express.

3. Accept the Texture of Your Voice

Maybe your voice cracks when you're nervous. Maybe it's soft. Maybe you speak slowly. That's okay. The goal isn't perfection — it's connection. And connection comes from sincerity.

Instead of fighting your voice, embrace it. Speak from your heart. People feel truth more than they hear polish.

4. Practice Speaking from the Soul

Whether in writing, conversations, or public speaking — practice letting your voice carry your emotions. Tell your story. Ask honest questions. Say "I don't know" when you're unsure. That vulnerability is your strength.

5. Protect Your Voice From Negativity

Not everyone will understand or support your voice — and that's normal. Some may criticize or mock you. Remember, their reaction says more about them than about you.

Stay rooted in your why. Surround yourself with those who value realness. Let your voice echo in safe places first — and then gradually, let it carry into the world.

You are not here to blend in. You are here to break the silence, to own your truth, and to inspire others with your journey.

So speak — even if your voice trembles. Because every time you honor your voice, you help someone else find theirs too.

21.4 Real-Life Practice: Speak Your Truth Challenge

It's one thing to think about expressing your truth — it's another to actually do it. This section is your invitation to take a bold, courageous step: to speak up, to share something real, and to start owning your story out loud. We call it the Speak Your Truth Challenge — not because it's easy, but because it's transformative.

This challenge is about small, real actions that bring you closer to yourself. Whether you're speaking up for yourself in a relationship, expressing your dream in front of a group, or simply writing your feelings down — this is your space to grow.

? Why Do This Challenge?

Because growth happens when we move beyond our fear of being misunderstood.

Because your silence doesn't protect you — it only hides your power.

Because someone out there is waiting to hear your story and feel less alone.

? Step 1: Identify Your Truth

Start by asking: What truth have I been holding back?

It could be:

A boundary you haven't communicated

A dream you've been scared to share

An opinion you've silenced in a group

A feeling you've buried inside

Write it down. Be honest with yourself. This truth is your starting point.

? Step 2: Choose a Safe Space to Express It

Your first attempt doesn't have to be public. You can start small. Choose a space that feels emotionally safe:

A private journal

A voice note to yourself

A trusted friend or mentor

A supportive social media post

A support group or community

The goal is not to impress anyone. It's to practice being you, without apology.

? Step 3: Speak or Write It Out Loud

Now, express that truth.

Example prompts:

"I've been feeling ___ lately, and I think I need to talk about it."

"I want to try ___ but I've been scared people will judge me."

"One thing I'm passionate about that I've never shared is..."

Let your heart guide your words. It doesn't have to be polished or perfect. It just has to be real.

? Step 4: Reflect on the Experience

After you've expressed your truth, pause and reflect:

How did it feel to finally say it?

Were you proud? Relieved? Nervous?

What did you learn about yourself through this?

Jot down your thoughts in a notebook or journal. This reflection will deepen your understanding and confidence.

? Step 5: Repeat with Bigger Truths

As you build comfort with smaller truths, challenge yourself to speak deeper ones:

Share a piece of your personal journey.

Advocate for something you believe in.

Ask for what you need in your relationships or work.

With each act, your voice gets stronger. Your truth becomes your foundation, not your secret.

Bonus Tip: Create a Truth-Telling Jar

Every time you speak a truth — big or small — write it on a slip of paper and drop it in a jar. Over time, you'll see just how powerful your voice has been. It becomes a visual reminder of your growth.

Remember:

This is not a one-time challenge. This is a lifelong practice. The more you speak your truth, the more free, confident, and aligned you'll feel.

Your voice matters.

Your truth matters.

You matter.

So go ahead — start with one sentence today. One moment of truth can change everything.

XVI
Managing Expectations

The Weight of Expectations

Have you ever felt like no matter what you do, it's never quite enough?

That feeling — the silent pressure pressing on your chest, the invisible checklist running in your head — is the weight of expectations.

From the moment we're born, expectations begin to surround us like invisible threads. Some are spoken:

"Get good marks."

"Be obedient."

"Don't fail."

Others are unspoken, passed down from family, culture, and society:

"You should be married by 25."

"You must have a stable career."

"You're the eldest — set an example."

And gradually, without even realizing it, we begin to measure our worth based on these outside voices. We begin to confuse expectations with our identity.

? But what happens when we can't live up to them?

We start feeling guilt, shame, fear, and self-doubt.

We ask ourselves questions like:

"Why can't I be like them?"

"What if I fail and disappoint everyone?"

"Am I falling behind in life?"

These are not your inner voice. These are the echoes of expectations placed on you — echoes that make you question your value when you don't meet someone else's standard.

? Expectations vs. Reality

There's a constant tug-of-war between where we are and where we're expected to be.

Maybe you've:

Chosen a different career than your parents hoped for.

Not yet settled down in a relationship.

Taken longer to find your purpose.

Decided not to follow the crowd.

And even though those choices feel right to you, that little voice still says, "But what will people say?"

This fear of judgment — of being misunderstood — often holds us back more than failure itself. We start to shrink, to silence our truth, just to fit in.

? But here's something you must know:

Expectations are not laws. They are opinions, often based on someone else's version of success.

And that version may not be meant for you.

What if your timing is different?

What if your path is not meant to be straight and predictable?

What if your dreams don't look like anyone else's?

That doesn't mean you're wrong. It means you're real.

? Releasing the Pressure

Recognizing the weight of expectations is the first step to freeing yourself from them. Ask yourself:

"Whose voice is this I'm trying to please?"

"Is this what I want, or what I think I should want?"

"If no one was watching, what would I do differently?"

Your answers may surprise you. They may scare you. But they will also guide you toward your truth.

?? Final Thought

You are not here to live a life that pleases everyone else.

You are here to live your life — messy, magical, evolving, and deeply authentic.

It's okay to set down the weight of unrealistic expectations.

It's okay to walk at your own pace.

And it's more than okay to redefine success for yourself.

Because your peace, your joy, your wholeness — they're worth more than any approval.

So breathe.

Let go.

And remind yourself: I am enough, just as I am.

22.2 When Expectations Hurt More Than Help

Expectations can be motivating — like the push that gets you out of bed when you feel like giving up. But sometimes, they don't feel like a gentle push. They feel like a heavy hand pressing down, telling you to run faster, do more, be better — constantly.

And instead of helping you grow, they start to quietly crush you.

? The Silent Damage

Let's be real — we all want to make our loved ones proud. We all want to achieve something meaningful. But the problem begins when expectations turn into silent pressure, whispering:

"You're behind."

"You're not good enough."

"Everyone else is doing better than you."

That's when expectation shifts from being a goal to being a burden. And over time, that burden can start to hurt you in ways you don't even notice until you're completely drained.

You begin to:

Doubt yourself constantly

Feel anxious about making mistakes

Overthink every decision

Work beyond your limits just to keep up appearances

And worst of all, you might start tying your self-worth to your performance. If you succeed, you feel okay. If you fail, you feel like a failure.

But your worth isn't tied to what you achieve. It never was.

? When It Comes From People You Love

The hardest part is when the pressure comes from people who genuinely care about you. Parents, mentors, teachers — they often mean well. But their expectations can unknowingly become a source of pain, especially when:

They project their own unfulfilled dreams onto you.

They define "success" in a narrow way.

They compare you to others, even subtly.

They don't understand your passions or choices.

It's not always about rebellion — sometimes it's about survival. About protecting your inner peace.

? Your Inner Critic Isn't Always Right

Sometimes the loudest expectations come from inside you.

Maybe you've internalized what others said and turned it into your own voice:

"I should always be strong."

"I can't rest until I prove myself."

"I must never fail."

But here's a gentle reminder: You are not a machine. You are human. And being human means allowing room for flaws, for breaks, for vulnerability.

Holding yourself to impossible standards only builds walls between who you are and who you're trying to be.

?? What You Can Do

Here's what healing looks like:

Recognize the pressure: Ask yourself what expectation is making you feel small or stressed.

Question its source: Did you choose it? Or did someone else?

Challenge the narrative: Who says you have to do it this way? What would you do differently?

Allow space for your truth: Your dreams, timelines, and values are valid — even if they don't match the norm.

? A Gentle Truth

Not every expectation is meant to be carried. Some are meant to be questioned. Others are meant to be released.

Letting go doesn't mean giving up — it means giving yourself permission to live fully, freely, and honestly.

You deserve a life that feels light, not one that constantly weighs on your soul.

22.3 Redefining Success on Your Own Terms

Have you ever paused and asked yourself: What does success mean to me — not to the world, not to my family, not to society — but to me?

So often, we inherit a definition of success that has nothing to do with our inner truth. It sounds like this:

A high-paying job.

A house by a certain age.

A "perfect" relationship.

Social media-worthy achievements.

And we chase it. Desperately. Without stopping to ask if we even want what we're running after.

? The Courage to Rethink Everything

Redefining success is not a rebellion. It's a return — to yourself. It's giving yourself permission to say:

"I don't want what everyone else wants."

"My version of success may look different — and that's okay."

"If it gives me peace, passion, and purpose, then it is enough."

For some, success is leading a team. For others, it's writing poetry, or teaching, or healing, or building something quietly that changes lives.

Success doesn't have to be loud to be real.

? Creating Your Own Definition

Here are a few questions to guide your journey inward:

What makes me feel fulfilled, not just busy?

What values do I want to live by — kindness, freedom, growth, creativity?

If I had no one to impress, what would I choose to do with my time?

What moments have made me feel truly alive?

Who am I outside of roles, titles, or expectations?

Your answers are your personal roadmap. Trust them.

?? Letting Go of Comparison

Redefining success means stepping off the comparison treadmill. You no longer need to measure your pace by someone else's progress.

Some people bloom early. Others bloom later. But every flower has its own season — and it doesn't rush or compete. It just grows.

So will you.

? Your Success Might Be...

Choosing peace over pressure.

Walking away from what doesn't serve you.

Starting over at 30, or 40, or 60.

Healing your past wounds.

Living a simple, joy-filled life.

And that is just as powerful as any medal or milestone.

♥? Final Thought

Success isn't a finish line. It's a feeling — of being aligned with your truth, of waking up each day proud of who you're becoming.

And here's the best part: you get to define it.

So don't let anyone shrink your story. Rewrite the rules if they no longer fit. This is your life — and that alone makes it worthy of your own, honest version of success.

22.4 Healing from Disappointment

Disappointment is that quiet ache in your chest when reality doesn't meet your hopes. It shows up when a plan fails, a person lets you down, or when life — despite your best efforts — just doesn't go your way.

And it hurts. Deeply.

Not because you're weak, but because you cared. Because you dared to hope. And when something you hoped for doesn't happen, it's natural to feel sad, frustrated, or even lost.

? The Emotional Weight of Disappointment

Sometimes we try to brush it off — "It's fine, I'll get over it."
But underneath, we may still be carrying:

A broken trust

A lost opportunity

A relationship that didn't work out

A dream that had to be put on hold

Unprocessed disappointment can quietly turn into self-doubt. We start to question:

"Was I not good enough?"

"Did I expect too much?"

"Am I just unlucky?"

But healing begins when you stop blaming yourself and allow space to feel what you're feeling — without shame.

? Let Yourself Grieve What Didn't Happen

Yes, you're allowed to grieve the version of life you imagined.
It's okay to cry. To sit with the sadness. To say, "This really hurt me." That's not weakness — it's honesty. And it's the first step toward release.

Just like a physical wound needs cleaning and care, emotional wounds need acknowledgment and love.

? Choose Healing, Gently

Here's how you can begin to heal from disappointment:

Write it out: Journaling can help release bottled-up emotions. Write what happened. How it made you feel. What you wish had been different.

Talk about it: Share with someone who listens without judgment — a friend, mentor, or therapist.

Practice self-kindness: You're not a failure because things didn't work out. You're still learning. Still growing.

Look for the lesson: Every disappointment carries a hidden insight — about life, people, and yourself.

Keep hope alive: One closed door doesn't mean they all are. Sometimes rejection is redirection — guiding you to something even better.

?? A Soft Reminder

Healing takes time. Don't rush it. There's no timeline for when you "should" feel okay.

Disappointment doesn't define you. It doesn't mean your dreams are over — just that the path might look different now.

You're allowed to outgrow what once fit you. You're allowed to start again.

And most of all — you're allowed to still believe in beautiful things.

22.5 Creating a Healthier Relationship with Your Goals

Goals are beautiful. They give us direction, inspire growth, and keep us moving. But when we tie our worth to outcomes, or chase goals out of fear, pressure, or comparison — they can turn heavy and hurtful.

It's time to create a new relationship with your goals. One that's kind, flexible, and rooted in your truth — not just in achievement.

? The Difference Between Hustle and Heart

There's a big difference between chasing goals because you love the journey — and chasing them because you're afraid of being "not enough" without them.

Ask yourself:

Am I doing this to prove something?

Am I trying to earn approval or love?

Or am I pursuing this because it aligns with who I am and what I value?

When goals are rooted in love — not fear — they energize rather than exhaust you.

? Letting Go of the All-or-Nothing Mindset

You are not a failure because a goal took longer than expected. You are not unworthy if a dream shifts or changes direction.

Life is not a straight line — and neither is growth. Sometimes you'll pause, pivot, or even completely start over. That's okay.

It's time to redefine what it means to "win":

Progress is a win.

Trying again is a win.

Resting is a win.

Choosing peace is a win.

? Make Your Goals More Gentle and More Powerful

Here's how to set goals that feel supportive, not suffocating:

Start with your 'Why': What is your deeper reason? Make it about growth, impact, or joy — not just the end result.

Break them down: Small, consistent steps often go farther than one giant leap.

Celebrate along the way: Don't wait for the finish line to feel proud. Every step matters.

Let goals evolve with you: You are allowed to change. So are your dreams.

Detach from perfection: Progress, not perfection, is the real path forward.

?♀? When Goals Meet Grace

You can be ambitious and gentle with yourself.
You can dream big and honor your limits.
You can strive for more without shaming where you are now.

Give your goals space to breathe. Let them grow with love, not pressure.

And remember: You are already whole — your goals are just the path you're dancing on.

With this, you've completed Chapter 22: Letting Go of the Old You.

XVII
Finding Your Voice and Owning It

Understanding What It Means to "Find Your Voice"

Your voice isn't just about the sound you make — it's about what you stand for, how you express your truth, and the courage to let your inner self be seen and heard.

Finding your voice means:

Speaking honestly even when it's hard.

Making choices aligned with your values.

23.2 Overcoming Fear of Judgment

Let's get real — the fear of judgment is one of the loudest reasons we stay silent.

We don't speak up not because we have nothing to say... but because we worry what people will think when we finally say it.

Will they laugh? Will they think I'm arrogant? Weak? Dramatic?

Will they roll their eyes behind my back? Or worse... walk away?

This fear — it's so deep, sometimes we don't even realize it's there. It hides behind our silence. Behind our "I'm fine." Behind our fake smiles and carefully curated posts. And the worst part? We start judging ourselves before anyone else gets a chance.

But here's the truth no one tells us loud enough: People's opinions are not your truth.

Everyone sees the world through their own lens — their upbringing, their insecurities, their limitations. So when they judge you, they're often projecting their own fears, not reflecting your worth.

If someone calls you "too much," maybe it's because they were never allowed to be fully themselves.

If someone calls you "too emotional," maybe they were taught to hide their own feelings.

If someone calls you "too ambitious," maybe they gave up on their own dreams long ago.

You are not too much. You are just enough — for the right people, in the right places, doing the right work.

So how do we begin to quiet the fear of judgment?

1. Acknowledge it without shame.

Say it out loud: "I am afraid of being judged." That honesty is the first crack in the wall. Hiding the fear gives it more power. Naming it shrinks it.

2. Ask yourself: What's the worst that could happen?

And then... what if it does happen? Will you survive a side-eye? A rude comment? A misunderstanding? Yes. You will. Your voice, your message, your truth — they're stronger than discomfort.

3. Focus on your "why."

Why do you want to speak? Why do you want to be heard? When your why becomes louder than your fear, your voice will rise. Every time. Speak for your younger self, for your future self, for those who still feel voiceless.

4. Remember: Everyone is being judged anyway.

No matter what you do, someone will have an opinion. So why not do what you believe in? Be judged for being real — not for playing small.

5. Create a safe space to practice.

Start by opening up to a journal. Then a trusted friend. Then a supportive room. One by one, like strength training for your soul, your voice grows louder and steadier.

The fear of judgment may never vanish completely — and that's okay. Courage isn't about the absence of fear. It's about choosing to show up anyway.

Let this be the moment you stop asking for permission to be seen and heard.

You're allowed to take up space. You're allowed to speak with feeling. You're allowed to be you.

Saying no when needed — and yes when it matters.

But for many of us, especially as women or youth, this voice was buried early — by expectations, judgment, fear, or trauma. You may have been told to be quiet, polite, or agreeable. You may have learned to silence yourself just to fit in or keep the peace.

This chapter is your invitation to unlearn all of that — and step back into your truth.

23.3 Speaking Authentically and with Confidence

Authenticity isn't about having all the right words or never messing up. It's about being real — showing up as yourself, flaws and all, and saying what you truly believe, even when your voice shakes.

When we speak authentically, we stop performing. We stop pretending. And we start connecting — deeply, honestly, and powerfully.

But let's be honest... it's scary.

You might worry:

"What if they don't get me?"

"What if I stumble?"

"What if I'm not enough?"

But what if... you are?

What if your story, your truth, your way of expressing it — is exactly what someone else needs to hear?

Let's break it down.

1. Speak from Your Heart, Not a Script

Confidence isn't about memorizing the perfect line. It's about trusting your heart. When you speak from lived experience, people feel it. You don't need fancy words. You need your words.

Instead of: "What should I say?"

Ask: "What do I honestly feel or believe?"

People connect with honesty more than perfection.

2. Own Your Story

You don't need to hide your past, your pain, or your journey. In fact, that's your power.

Your voice gains strength every time you share something real — whether it's a lesson you learned, a boundary you created, or a moment you grew through.

Confidence isn't about never being broken — it's about showing how you put yourself back together.

3. Practice Out Loud

Yes, literally — speak in front of a mirror. Record voice notes. Talk to your journal. Confidence comes from doing, not just thinking.

Every time you speak your truth out loud, even in private, your voice gets more comfortable being heard. You become your own safest listener.

4. Breathe Into the Moment

When we're nervous, we hold our breath — and that tightens everything, including our voice.

So before you speak:

Inhale deeply.

Pause.

Exhale slowly.

Then speak from that grounded place.

You'll feel more present, and your voice will feel more rooted — in truth and peace.

5. Let Go of Needing to Be Liked

This is a hard one, but vital. Not everyone will understand or agree with you — and that's okay. You're not here to please everyone. You're here to be you.

The more you try to water down your voice, the less power it carries. Speak for the people who are meant to hear you — and let the rest go.

6. Confidence Grows With Every Step

You don't need to be the loudest voice in the room to be the most powerful. You just need to be honest. Speak even if your hands tremble. Speak even if your voice cracks. That's how strength builds — moment by moment.

You may not feel "ready" — do it anyway.

You may not be "perfect" — speak anyway.

You may not get applause — keep showing up anyway.

Because every time you speak with authenticity, you prove to yourself: My voice matters.

And that, dear soul, is where unshakable confidence begins.

23.4 Creating Safe Spaces for Self-Expression

Before you can express yourself freely, you need to feel safe — not just physically, but emotionally and mentally too. Without safety, your voice stays guarded. Your truth stays silent.

That's why creating a safe space — for yourself and for others — is not a luxury. It's a necessity.

You don't bloom in chaos. You bloom in calm. In spaces where you're not judged, mocked, or rushed. In spaces where you can unfold gently, honestly, and without fear of being misunderstood.

So how do we begin to create such spaces?

1. Create Safety Within Yourself First

Your inner voice sets the tone.

If you constantly criticize yourself — "That was stupid," "Why did I say that?" — you're creating an unsafe space within. You won't feel free to speak if you're your own biggest bully.

Start by becoming your own ally:

Practice self-compassion: Speak to yourself the way you would to a friend.

Let go of perfection: It's okay to not always have the right words.

Give yourself permission: To mess up, to grow, to learn out loud.

When your inner world becomes softer, more forgiving — you become braver.

2. Surround Yourself With Supportive People

Not everyone deserves a front-row seat to your growth. Some people listen to reply. Others listen to judge. But a few — the special ones — listen to understand. They hold your truth gently.

Choose those people.

Notice how you feel around them. Do you shrink or expand?

Do they allow you to be messy? Vulnerable? Real?

Can you speak without rehearsing?

If yes — that's your safe space. Protect it. Nurture it. Be that safe space for them, too.

3. Set Boundaries to Protect Your Voice

Boundaries aren't walls — they're doors. They don't shut people out. They guide people in.

Let others know how you wish to be treated when you're sharing something sensitive.

Say things like:

"I'm not looking for advice right now, just a listening ear."

"This is hard for me to talk about — please hold it with care."

"Can we keep this just between us?"

Your voice deserves to be heard with respect. Boundaries create that respect.

4. Create a Ritual for Self-Expression

It could be journaling with soft music, voice-recording your thoughts, painting your feelings, or having a weekly heart-to-heart with a friend.

When you create a ritual around expression, you give your voice a sacred space. A rhythm. A routine. You show your heart: You matter. Your truth matters.

5. Be a Safe Space for Others

Want more safe spaces? Become one. When someone opens up to you, don't interrupt. Don't fix. Just be present.

Hold their words like you'd hold a butterfly — gently, patiently, with awe.

When we start holding space for each other, the whole world begins to feel a little safer. A little softer.

At the end of the day, creating a safe space for self-expression is an act of deep love — for yourself and for others. And when safety exists, courage follows. Truth follows. Healing follows.

Because in a safe space, your voice doesn't just speak.
It sings.

XVIII
Embracing Growth and Uncertainty

Life doesn't come with a map. And growth never follows a straight line.

Sometimes, we think we're finally "getting there," only to feel lost again the next day. One moment we're sure of who we are — the next, everything changes. That's not failure. That's growth.

Growth is messy. Uncertainty is uncomfortable. But both are necessary if you want to evolve into the person you're meant to be.

24.1 The Nature of Growth

Growth is a word we often hear, but rarely stop to understand. We associate it with progress, success, milestones. But true growth? It's not always glamorous. It's often invisible. It's a quiet, personal revolution that happens deep within.

Real growth doesn't always look like winning.
Sometimes, it looks like:

Saying no when you used to say yes just to please others.

Walking away from a friendship that once meant everything but now drains your peace.

Crying because you finally let yourself feel something you've avoided for years.

Starting over — even when it terrifies you.

Growth is not a final destination. It's not something you arrive at one day and say, "I'm done." It's a continuous, evolving journey — a lifelong unfolding of who you are, who you were, and who you're meant to be.

Growth is Often Uncomfortable

Let's be honest. Growth hurts. It stretches us beyond our comfort zones. It forces us to confront uncomfortable truths about ourselves. It challenges our habits, tests our patience, and brings up insecurities we thought we buried.

And that's why many people resist growth.

Because change is uncomfortable.

Because familiarity feels safer than possibility.

But here's the truth: comfort is not always your friend. Sometimes, it's the cage that keeps you from flying.

Every time you feel stuck, confused, or out of place — consider that it may be a sign:

You're growing. And that discomfort? It means something inside you is shifting, evolving, preparing you for something new.

Growth is Silent Before It's Visible

A seed doesn't bloom overnight. It spends weeks — even months — hidden beneath the soil, building roots, gathering strength. That's what your growth looks like, too.

People may not notice it.

You may not even notice it.

But every day you:

Choose healing over hiding,

Choose reflection over reaction,

Choose truth over approval —

You are growing.

The results may not be instant. But trust: the transformation is happening.

You Outgrow, You Rebuild, You Rise

As you grow, you will outgrow people. Places. Old dreams. Old versions of yourself.

This is normal. This is healthy.

You may look back at someone you once were — naive, broken, bitter, scared — and feel a strange mix of love and sorrow. Let yourself feel it. That version of you survived long enough to bring you here. Don't shame them. Thank them.

Then let them go.

And in their place, welcome the you who is wiser. Softer. Braver. More aligned.

Growth is Personal — and No One Else Has to Understand It

Not everyone will understand your journey. Some people may question why you've changed. Why you've become quieter. Stronger. More distant. Or more honest.

You don't owe anyone an explanation.

Your growth is yours. Your healing is yours. Your choices are yours. And you are allowed to rewrite your story as many times as you need to — even if no one else understands the chapters you left behind.

Final Thought

So if today feels confusing, heavy, uncertain — pause. Breathe. And say to yourself:

"I may not know exactly where I'm going, but I trust the process. I trust myself. I am not lost. I am growing."

Because the truth is:

Growth is not about changing who you are — it's about coming home to who you've always been.

24.2 Why Uncertainty is a Sign of Progress

Uncertainty is one of the most uncomfortable feelings in the world. It creeps in when the path ahead isn't clear. When you've outgrown the old, but the new hasn't fully arrived. It's that strange in-between space — the unknown.

But what if I told you... uncertainty isn't your enemy? What if I told you that uncertainty is proof that you are evolving?

Yes — read that again.

Uncertainty Means You're Moving

When we're stuck in routines, patterns, or identities that no longer serve us, we feel certain.

Because we know what to expect.

Even if we're unhappy, it's familiar.

Even if we're unfulfilled, it's predictable.

But the moment you start questioning things...

The moment you start asking,

"What do I really want?"

"Is this the life I'm meant for?"

"Who am I becoming?"

That's the moment your soul begins to stir.

That's the moment change begins.

And naturally, with change comes uncertainty.
It means you're stepping into something new.
It means your spirit is no longer willing to shrink just to feel safe.

Clarity Doesn't Always Come First

We wait for clarity like it's a bus that will arrive and take us somewhere magical.

But often, clarity doesn't come before the journey — it comes during it. Or even after.

You don't have to have it all figured out to begin.

Sometimes, you just have to take one honest step — in faith, in fear, in confusion — and trust that the ground will meet your feet.

Let yourself be a beginner.

Let yourself be unsure.

Because growth doesn't require perfection — it only asks for courage.

Uncertainty Creates Openness

When you don't know what's next, you become open.
Open to new ideas.
Open to new paths.
Open to discovering parts of yourself you never knew existed.

That openness? That's magic.

It's how you stumble upon dreams you never thought you'd dare to chase.

It's how you meet people who help you grow.
It's how you discover that you are far more capable, resilient, and brave than you ever imagined.

The Cocoon is Meant to Be Dark

Think of a caterpillar becoming a butterfly. There's a time when it's inside the cocoon — no longer who it was, not yet who it will be. It's messy. Confusing. Completely unrecognizable.

But that dark space is necessary.
Because that's where transformation happens.

You are allowed to be in your own cocoon right now.
You are allowed to not know what's next.
You are allowed to sit in the discomfort of not having answers.

This doesn't mean you're behind.

This means you're becoming.

Final Thought

The next time you feel uncertain, instead of panicking — pause and whisper to yourself:

"This feeling means I'm alive. This feeling means I'm growing. I am on the edge of something new."

Let uncertainty be your sign — not of failure, but of unfolding.

Because progress isn't always clear-cut or confident.

Sometimes, it feels like doubt.

Sometimes, it feels like fear.

But it's still progress.

Keep going.

24.3 Letting Go of Old Versions of You

There comes a time in life when you realize — you're not who you used to be.

You've grown. You've learned. You've shed layers.

And yet, a part of you still clings to the past — to an older version of yourself.

That version may feel familiar.

It may be the you who played small to keep others comfortable.

The you who was scared to ask for what you needed.

The you who settled because you didn't yet believe you were worthy of more.

But now? You're not her anymore.

And it's okay — more than okay — to let her go.

Why It's Hard to Let Go

It's difficult to release our past selves, not because we want to stay there, but because those old versions helped us survive.

They protected us. Adapted for us.

They were born from circumstances — pain, loss, heartbreak, fear — that shaped us.

To let go of them feels like a betrayal. But it isn't.

Letting go doesn't mean you hate who you were.

It means you finally love yourself enough to evolve.

You can hold compassion for who you were... and still outgrow her.

You're Allowed to Change

Sometimes people around you will say:

"You've changed."

"You're different now."

"Why aren't you the same anymore?"

And maybe they'll say it like it's a bad thing.

But here's your gentle reminder:

You're not here to remain the same.

You're here to transform, again and again, into deeper, freer, truer versions of yourself.

You're allowed to leave behind beliefs that no longer serve you.

You're allowed to heal from things that used to define you.

You're allowed to want different things — softer things, stronger things, realer things.

You Can Grieve and Grow at the Same Time

Letting go of an old version of yourself is a kind of grief.

You're saying goodbye to who you were — even if she was hurting, even if she was lost.

There may be tears. There may be nostalgia. There may be moments when you miss her.

That's okay.

Grief doesn't cancel growth.

You can feel sadness and still step forward.

You can hold space for both the pain of the past and the promise of what's next.

You are not weak for feeling both.

You are whole.

Final Thought

So here's your permission, in case you needed it:

You are allowed to rewrite your story.

You are allowed to begin again.

You are allowed to let go of the girl who got you through the storm — and become the woman who builds the sunshine.

Letting go isn't forgetting.

It's remembering with love, and choosing to live with freedom.

The next chapter of your life is calling.

And it needs this version of you — the one who's not afraid to grow.

24.4 Choosing Growth Even When It's Lonely

Growth is beautiful. Empowering. Liberating.

But let's be honest — growth can also feel incredibly lonely.

When you begin to change, not everyone will understand you.

Not everyone will cheer for you.

Not everyone will walk with you into your next chapter.

And that's a pain people don't talk about enough.

When You Outgrow Spaces and People

You might find yourself no longer relating to the conversations you used to enjoy.

You might start feeling out of place in rooms that once felt like home.

You may notice that the people you once leaned on don't feel as safe anymore.

It's confusing. Because nothing terrible happened — but everything's different.

And the truth is: sometimes when you grow, you outgrow.

Not out of arrogance. Not out of pride. But because your soul is expanding.

And not every person or place can meet you in that expansion.

It's not your fault. It's not theirs either.

It's just a sign of movement — and maturity.

Growth Requires Solitude

There will be seasons when you walk alone.

Where your Friday nights are spent journaling instead of partying.

Where your heart is healing quietly, away from noise and distractions.

Where you have to be your own motivator, your own safe space, your own best friend.

And in those moments, you might wonder,

"Is it worth it?"

Let me tell you: yes.

Because solitude isn't the same as emptiness.

Solitude is sacred.

It's where you meet your most authentic self.

It's where you learn your strength.

It's where the whispers of your purpose become loud enough to hear.

The People Who Get It Will Find You

You won't always be this alone.

The more you grow, the more aligned you become.

And as you step into your truth, you'll start to attract people who see you — the real you.

People who don't just tolerate your growth, but celebrate it.

People who bring peace, not pressure.

But they'll come only when you've made room.

And sometimes, the room is made by letting go of what no longer fits.

So trust the loneliness — not as punishment, but as preparation.

You Are Not Doing This in Vain

Every boundary you set...

Every time you choose rest instead of burnout...

Every time you walk away from something comfortable but misaligned...

You are planting seeds for a better life.

Even if no one claps for you right now.

Even if no one understands your path.

Clap for yourself.

Understand yourself.

Hold your vision, even in the silence.

Because the world may not get it yet — but you do. And that's enough.

Final Thought

Choosing growth can feel like walking through a forest with no map. It's dark. It's unfamiliar. It's lonely.

But one day, you'll look around and realize... you made it through. And not only that — you bloomed.

So don't stop.

Even when it's lonely, keep walking.

Because what's ahead of you is worth every step.

And so are you.

25.1 Walking With Courage: A Final Talk

Dear reader,

If you've reached this chapter, I want you to pause for a moment — truly pause — and honour yourself. Do you realise how much courage it takes to face your pain, your questions, your silence, and still keep reading, still keep showing up?

This book was not designed to give you answers wrapped in bows. It was built from tears, hope, grit, and the desire to let you know — someone understands. And most importantly, someone believes in you.

In these pages, we walked together. Through wounds that may still ache. Through victories that may have gone unnoticed by the world but changed everything within you. Through the heavy and the healing. You've met versions of yourself you had forgotten or were afraid to acknowledge.

And now, as we close this chapter, let me whisper this:

You are no longer standing in the same place where you started. Even if your surroundings haven't changed much... you have.

You are no longer confused — not because life has become easy, but because you've become wiser.

25.2 Your Power Is Not in Perfection — It's in Progress

Let this sink in deeply: Your power was never meant to be perfect. It was never about being flawless, always strong, or never crying. It was about staying — staying with your truth, staying with your healing, staying with your dream, even when it hurt.

Progress is quiet. Sometimes invisible. It happens in those small moments when you say, "I won't give up." It's found in the courage to rest without guilt. In the strength to ask for help. In the decision to forgive, not because they deserve it, but because you do.

You don't have to fix your whole life overnight.

All you need is to believe that your journey matters — that each small, shaky, faithful step counts.

And yes, sometimes progress means falling apart and gently putting yourself back together — softer, but stronger. More broken, but more real. More tired, but more alive.

25.3 A Letter to Your Future Self

Now, I invite you to connect with your future — the woman or young soul you are becoming.

This isn't just a reflection. It's a legacy. A conversation between your now and your next.

Take a pen or open your journal, and begin:

"Dear Future Me,

I hope you still remember where you came from.

I hope you never silence your voice to make others comfortable.

I hope you wear your story like a crown — not because it was easy, but because you rose through it anyway.

I hope you forgive faster, laugh louder, and never forget that you are your own home.

If you're ever unsure, remember this version of us — still trying, still hoping, still showing up."

And when you're done writing, hold that letter close. Because no matter how much life changes, your words will bring you back to who you truly are.

25.4 A Final Whisper: You Are the Author Now

Now, the story is yours to write — every word, every pause, every new chapter. You've carried this book with you through your heart's valleys and mountains. But now, it's time to set it down and live.

You are not the victim of your past — you are the voice of your future.

Your story matters. Your dreams are valid. And your presence in this world — yes, your presence — is needed more than you know.

So I leave you with this:

Speak with conviction. Love without apology. Rest without guilt. Choose peace without explanation. And chase your truth like your life depends on it — because it does.

No more waiting for someone else to write your happy ending.

You are the writer.

You are the fire.

You are the light.

And you are just beginning.

Final Reflection Prompt: Your Empowerment Pledge

Take a few minutes to declare your truth. Let it be your closing ceremony — a vow to yourself.

Write this:

I am no longer available for:

____

I now choose to welcome:

____

I promise to my soul:

____

Sign your name. Date it. Frame it if you like.

Let it be your personal contract — the one you never break again.

And when life gets noisy, come back here. To this moment. To this version of you who chose hope.

With fierce belief in you,

With love as real as your story,

Pushpa Bhatti

Remember, your mind is a powerful tool. When you learn to question your negative thoughts instead of accepting them blindly, you gain control over your inner dialogue. This exercise is a step toward reclaiming your peace and confidence, one thought at a time.

Becoming You

You began in a fog, unsure and small,
With questions that echoed, no answers at all.
A heart full of wonder, a mind full of fear,
You carried your chaos, year after year.
    You fell and you stumbled, cried through the night,
But still, you stood up — still chose to fight.
No one could see it, the war deep inside,
But you kept on walking with trembling pride.
    You healed in silence, you bloomed unseen,
You cleaned up the wreckage of who you had been.
You learned to love slow, and trust again too,
You whispered forgiveness — first to you.
    You are not the scars, nor the pieces you've lost,
You are what survived, no matter the cost.
You're fire and gentle, you're storm and the sky,
You're laughter and longing, you're learning to fly.
    So here you are now, at the edge of the page,
A warrior in stillness, a queen through the rage.
Don't close this book thinking it's done —
You're only beginning, you've only begun.

Affirmation Page: I Choose Me

Repeat these aloud. Write them down. Let them live in your heart.

? I am no longer waiting for permission — I am giving it to myself.

? I embrace my journey, even the messy parts.

? My confusion was not weakness; it was a sign I was growing.

? I am not behind — I am blooming right on time.

? I release what no longer serves me, and I welcome peace.

? I choose progress over perfection, always.

? My voice matters. My dreams are valid. My soul is worthy.

? I forgive myself for what I didn't know before.

? I am allowed to take up space, to rest, to rise, to begin again.

? I am powerful, grounded, evolving — and still soft.

? I am not alone. I am deeply connected to my purpose.

? I will show up for myself, even when it's hard.

? I am not confused anymore.

? I am becoming — and I love who I'm becoming.

Thank You, Dear Reader

Dear You,

Thank you.

Not just for picking up this book, but for holding space for yourself within its pages.

Thank you for being brave enough to sit with the confusion, the heaviness, the questions.

Thank you for allowing my words to touch your soul, for walking through your own shadows with honesty, and for choosing yourself — again and again.

You didn't just read this book.

You felt it.

You lived it.

You gave it meaning with your tears, your thoughts, your silent nods in the middle of the night.

This book may have been written by me, but its real power came alive in you — in your openness, your resilience, your journey.

You are the heartbeat behind these pages.

You are the reason this book exists.

I wrote this to remind you of your light, but somewhere along the way, you reminded me of mine, too.

Keep growing. Keep breaking patterns. Keep walking toward your truth, no matter how uncertain it feels.

You are not alone — not now, not ever.

I'm cheering for you. Always.

With all my heart,

Pushpa Bhatti

Author. Sister. Believer in You.

9 79 8 8 9 9 8 4 7 8 8 2